Playground

John Buell

PLAYGROUND

Farrar, Straus and Giroux
New York

Copyright © 1976 by John Buell Associates Ltd.

All rights reserved

First printing, 1976

Printed in the United States of America

Published simultaneously in Canada

by McGraw-Hill Ryerson Ltd., Toronto

Designed by Dorris Huth

Library of Congress Cataloging in Publication Data

Buell, John.

Playground.

I. Title.

PZ4.B93P13 [PR9199.3.B766]   813'.5'4   75–35630

Playground

1

His holidays began at 5 a.m. He awoke a few minutes ahead of time, turned the alarm button off, and got up quietly not to disturb his wife in the other bed. He walked barefooted along the carpeted hall, past his son's room, then his daughter's, and down the wide turning stairs, also carpeted, through the large living room, which was strewn, he noticed, with last night's leavings: newspapers, magazines, cups, glasses, plates, a pizza box, his son's shoes, the constant domestic debris. He continued downstairs to the basement, still following the carpeted trail, and shut himself in the washroom and shaved and showered and woke up more fully and came out to put on the clothes he had laid out the night before. They were outdoor clothes, soft denim pants with a strong belt, a long-sleeved sport shirt, campers, and a green and black bush shirt which he carried upstairs to the kitchen and draped over a chair. 5:20, on schedule. He wound his watch.

He made and ate breakfast: orange juice, an egg, toast, instant coffee. It was too early for the morning paper. He turned the radio on low, hoping to get a weather report, but the night man was still on, reading baseball scores in a shushing voice. He lit a cigarette to sip the coffee with and checked his keys, wallet, licenses, money, credit cards, glasses. The light grew brighter outside the two kitchen windows, the sun would soon be all the way up. When he finished the coffee, he turned off the radio and put his dirty dishes in the washer but didn't turn it on. 5:35 now. He grabbed the woolen shirt in passing and went downstairs again and through a decorated metal door into the garage.

It held two cars, a Dodge Polara, his wife's, and a loaded Chrysler station wagon. It was cool in there. He worked his shirt on as he edged around the wagon for a last inspection. Everything seemed in place. The roof rack had canvas bags held down by a tarp and laced over with four stretch-fasteners. The inside was crammed with boxes, more canvas bags, camping and fishing gear, two tents, frozen food in Styrofoam containers, and all of it was covered with a vinyl sheet to discourage theft. On the front passenger seat were two side-opening duffel bags and on the floor a case of Bell's Scotch, twenty years old. The wagon was overloaded, but the engineers at his company had worked out safety margins for him: extra springs, shocks, anti-sway bar, oversized tires, air pressures, load distribution. He examined a check list, saw that no item was left open, and put it in his shirt pocket. He went to the garage door, pressed a starting button, and the door went up.

The dawn light was now strong, not yet warm. The sun was up somewhere but he couldn't see it. The large lawns of the neighborhood were still in deep shadow and his son's red Volkswagen was blocking the driveway.

He went back inside, searched on the kitchen table, found nothing, and went upstairs to his son's room. The young man in bed stirred. He poked on the dresser and found the keys.

"Your car's in my way, Tom, I'm taking your keys."

"Huh? Oh. Sorry. I . . ."

"Yeah."

As he left the room, the sleepy voice said, "Hope you make it with the fish. See you."

"See you."

He felt his muscle tone drop a little, he had tried to get his son to go with him. There had been no quarrel, just his expectation and his son's apparent indifference, a subtle pain. But he was used to it, he thought.

He went to his own bedroom and looked in.

"Betty."

"Hmmm."

"I'm going now."

She opened her eyes and lifted a hand. "Have a good time out there."

"Yeah. See you in two weeks."

"Bye."

"Bye."

He returned to the driveway and moved the Volkswagen, impossibly trying to not make noise, and put the keys on the kitchen table. He backed the wagon out, ignoring the seat-belt buzzer until he had closed the garage door and settled himself comfortably behind the wheel. He adjusted the mirrors, checked the gauges, put his cigarettes next to him on the seat, and eased the wagon past his lawn and into the wide curving street. He was started. It was 6 a.m., more or less still on schedule, as if that were important. You can't just leave, he mused, not angrily, there's always something to get in the way, domestic barbed wire.

He put on sunglasses, Bausch and Lomb G-15's, the pilot's kind, for he'd be facing the sun. He lit a cigarette, aware that he smoked too much, and tried to begin the long task of relaxing. But his face retained a worried tough cast, the complicated look of experience and authority. He was in his late forties, tall, filled out, big rather than fat, with plentiful hair modernized into sideburns and curling at the neck. He had a long face, heavy cheekbones, a few deep lines across the forehead, narrow brown eyes under the glasses, and a firm mouth that curved slightly upward at the corners and suggested irony more than humor.

He didn't notice the route, just that it was empty of traffic and fresh with new sunlight. He got out of the residential windings of Baie d'Urfé, took 2 & 20 going east to Montreal, something he did every working day, and stayed on the expressway through the city, crossed Champlain Bridge, followed the St. Lawrence until the city disappeared, and got on the road to Quebec City.

6

There wasn't much traffic at that hour, a few long trucks making time, speeders appearing at what seemed like regular intervals, but no tail-gaters, no jammed lanes, and no packs. They'd come later. It was Thursday in late June, too early in the season for the tourists and campers and workers on vacation. He was able to stay in the right lane for long stretches and didn't have to watch his mirrors all the time. But he still wasn't relaxing. He regarded driving as work that had to be professionally done, like flying. He stayed alert constantly, aware of every access road, every curve, every rise that blocked his view, the added momentum of going downhill, the quarter-mile buffer fore and aft, safe and unsafe crash spots along the sides of the throughway, the state of traffic ahead and behind. Things were done consciously and efficiently. He tried to run his life, life, that way. Even this holiday had been planned logistically, with three friends, over winter months, planned with a deep hunger for getting away, a need to remove themselves from the complex pressures of their work and lives. They studied maps, made check lists and schedules, got every piece of equipment in working order, spent—collectively—a little over two thousand dollars on new gear and clothing, and tried to organize contingencies out of the plan so that when they arrived they would have nothing to do but enjoy themselves fishing, drinking, eating, sleeping, all outdoors in rugged bush country. The efficient planning was also a form of dreaming. He sensed it, but it went largely unnoticed because they had the affluence and resources to make it happen.

He went 80 for nearly an hour and then slowed for the getting-to-work traffic, the blue-collar rush. It had an atmosphere of its own, it tended to stay in line and seemed to be made up mainly of older cars and small trucks. It poured in from the smaller towns and the countryside and headed for the bigger centers to make its living. Younger men, not yet patient with routine, did the passing and speeding, nudging the steadier traffic out of their way. Mobility, he thought, remembering reports and books and briefings, it speeded up people, made them do more things and faster, created new needs, new economies, new crimes, and . . . the heck with it, it's time to go fishing. But he was aware that he was doing that by means of a big wagon powered by a 440 cu. in. engine and loaded with holiday technology. So I'm aware, he argued with himself, everybody's aware these days, it doesn't have to mean anything. Aware of what? The traffic was beginning to thin and he was getting ready to start passing. It's no time for analysis, just enjoy it.

An hour later, when it was 8:35, he was in the white-collar traffic that would end up in Quebec City. As soon as he could he got off the throughway, pulled in at a service-station-and-restaurant, organized a coffee, a cigarette, and sat watching the flow of cars some two hundred yards away. There was something particular about his present position, and he was aware again. If he'd been on a business trip he would have stayed in the traffic, or, having pulled out, would have wanted to get back in. But now he was regarding it as something to get out of, something he shouldn't have been in at all. It was like a stampede of horsepower. Enormous energy getting people to work—and from it later— regulated by pavement and clock. And not a person in sight, only dimly seen drivers. His awareness made him uncomfortable, it was sudden and new, so it seemed, and there was something wrong. I once liked this. What ever made me think I liked it? I was young, younger, I didn't notice it. And now, now I'm . . . The heck with it, I'm going fishing. You shouldn't make problems out of everything. That's for philosophers. A temporary semi-humorous shrug-off. He knew he'd get back to it, or it to him. Efficiency. Let's go fishing first.

He thought of the next lap on his route, ordered more coffee, and reviewed what he had to do. It was unnecessary, but he enjoyed doing it, especially the idea that he was able to do it. He was an advance party of one, going ahead to prepare a campsite, the others would join him on Saturday, depending on flying conditions. The long-range forecast was good, but they had no local stations in the wilderness and you had to be your own meteorologist. This was to be no guided tour, they had picked an untouched lake in north-central Quebec, a complete change.

At 9:00 he got back on the less busy throughway and crossed the bridge into the city. At a choice of roads a while later, which would take him to 73N toward Lac St. Jean, he felt the binding logic of wheel and pavement and clock and their resultant scheduling which he was obeying, and slowed down to 30 and decided, no, I don't have to, and chose to see the sights of Quebec City. It was a small, private, subjective rebellion, nothing dramatic, a mild assertion of freedom, a willfulness perhaps, an insignificant shuffling of plans, his own plans at that. As he turned off the freeway he felt he was getting away with something. He was able to go slow, to look at things with curiosity, turn idly into any street, tell himself credibly that he was on vacation. His side trip took about two hours—he liked the historical sites, history made him feel he had come out on top—but he thought of it as having lost time, deliberately, and by choice, yes, but lost, as if time were a thing and had an ideal use.

By 11:08, according to his watch, he had circled the city and returned to the same freeway and the choice of roads and went north on 73N, which later became 175. By noon he was inside Laurentide Park. From the road he couldn't see any of the cabins or tent sites or the campers and trailers at *les campings*. They were probably down by the lakes. At Grand Lac Jacques-Cartier he pulled over to watch the scenery and to have two pre-lunch drinks from one of Bell's squat bottles, using a whiskey glass he kept in the dash, and at what seemed to be the town's only restaurant he had soup and roast beef, reheated but still rare, and surprisingly good. From 175 he forked northwest to 189, making a mental note to explore Portes de L'Enfer on the way back, and stopped and looked for fish at three of the rivers he was crossing and deliberately lost time and had more Bell's. It was beginning to feel like a holiday.

In mid-afternoon he was on 169 going west on the south shore of Lac St. Jean through Chambord and Val

Jalbert and Roberval and finally St. Felicien when he decided he had done enough driving for the day and pulled in at the best motel he could find on the west side. The Chrysler and the way he looked got him deferential treatment, which he took for granted, and a few dollars' tip bought him security for the wagon and space in the motel freezer for his food.

He brought one of the duffel bags, a flat briefcase, and the Bell's into the motel room. He felt immediately that he should phone his office. Maybe it was the briefcase or the motel, and even after he realized he didn't have to, he was tempted to do it anyway. It didn't feel right not having to phone somebody, or read reports, or go to a meeting, or see people over lunch. He went out for ice and made a drink. He was in a vacuum of unoccupied time. He undressed, showered, dressed again, in slip-on shoes instead of the campers. The stopover hadn't been in his plans, he still had about 150 miles to go by car. He thought of phoning home, but didn't. No one knew where he was, no one could reach him, and lines of communication were important. But this wasn't business, it was leisure, no one had to reach him, no one should try. Get away from it all, and stay away, that was the idea. Besides, tomorrow they'd know where you are, back on plan.

He regretted stopping. And having stopped on the way. There had been no reason for it, no purpose. It didn't accomplish anything, he hadn't really enjoyed it, and it left him in a motel with nothing to do. He tried to take a nap, and knew it was no good, he was still in transit and now behind schedule. The schedul-

ing had been a way of avoiding this. Avoiding what?—
he ducked away from the inquiry by getting up and going out. He walked the town a little, on Rue Principale,
where the only activity was, visited two bars but found
no one to really talk to, a few remarks about fishing to a
bartender, nothing to the two girls who looked him
over—the outdoor clothes weren't work clothes, a
sportsman—then late supper at the motel, where defer-
ence was already established, and finally back to the
room and the Bell's. He turned on the TV—a Los An-
geles P.I. show dubbed in France—and under its stay-
on-the-surface noise he studied the maps and the aeronautical chart he took from the briefcase. When he began nodding, from the long day and the liquor and the
boredom, he went to bed. Tomorrow had begun.

2

He was back on another schedule the next day, and he felt great, he told himself. He had a destination and plenty to do. Maybe the stopover had done him good after all, a rest is a rest, even if you don't like it. He left at 8 a.m., going northwest through Chibougamau Park, feeling better all the time. The country grew noticeably wilder, more challenging, and it made sense of the outdoor equipment, the ten-inch boots he was now wearing, the clothes, the tone of rugged sports. He responded to it by pushing the car a little harder, driving with conscious effort as though the wagon were a jeep, a hint of the boy pretending. He knew that it was, of course, a pose—he was too aware to deceive himself—but he was enjoying it, it was harmless. He brought the wagon to 80 on the two-lane road, and chuckled, and after a quick burst of speed he let it settle to a saner 70. At work, technology was taken solemnly, here it could be played with. Elapsed time from launch: 28 hours 17 minutes, and—he didn't want to take his eyes off the road for too long—something seconds. 10:17 EDT. Roger. He held his cigarette in a cupped hand and took deep manly drags. The road kept pointing to the mountains and clouds on the horizon and beyond, and he felt he was being released.

At last, near noon, he was entering Chibougamau. He went slowly along the short main street, down almost to walking speed, trying to savor the moment of arrival. It was a working town, full of trucks and older cars and men in work clothes, some few new streets laid out straight and square, a modern frontier community trying to urbanize itself. It was the end of the line for this part of Quebec. Beyond it was wild country, a vast bush with thousands of lakes, some enormous, many unnamed and unmapped, a sportsman's paradise, so it seemed, and uninhabited save for the Indians the government was still trying to technologize. It was untouched nature, regarded as raw and untamed, with fighting trout at least ten pounds heavy and as long as your arm. Months of planning and dreaming.

He drove barely a mile to the eastern edge of town, which bordered Gilman Lake and where two amphibious Cessnas were moored. He came to a studied stop, tasting the moment, in front of a row of connected buildings: a two-story house, which was also a store, a machine shop, and a large three-door garage that could accommodate trucks and small aircraft. The only sign was the gasoline brand on the fuel pumps. The entire place was run by three brothers and their families,

14

Richard, Henri, and Luc Tétrault, who were outfitters, carpenters, machinists, mechanics, flyers, and guides when they had the time. Their only capital, with third-grade educations, had been their energy and skills, and they were the envy of the small community, who explained it all as luck. He tapped the horn musically and left the keys on the dash.

A boy of six poked his head out of the screen door and darted back in. He burst out again, followed by a tall thin man in his late thirties.

"R'garde donc ça," said the man, smiling broadly, *"c'est monsieur Morison, y'est arrivé!"* Then in English, "Hello, Mr. Morison, hello." He had only a trace of a French accent. His enthusiasm was genuine, he liked his work. The boy went to the wagon and gawked at it.

"Hello, Henri. Yeah, I made it all right."

He had tried to get Henri to call him Spence, but the relationship stayed at Henri-and-Mister-Morison. They were in different worlds, as they both well knew, not bridgeable merely by an interest in fishing. Henri's way of life was Morison's recreation, one man's work was the other man's sport, a pastime that took as much capital as a small business. No resentment, just the difference. And Henri had no way of knowing how much Morison admired the enterprise and achievement of these men.

"I see the Cessna's okay," Morison said.

"Oh yeah, right on time. That a new Chrysler?"

"Yeah, reinforced for that load."

"They did a good job, she's riding nice and high."

"How's the fishing?"

"Hey, terrific. That big." He held his arms out full length and laughed. "You ready to go now?"

Morison laughed. "Yeah, but there's no hurry. I'm going to get a bite to eat."

"You want to eat with us, we're just sitting down."

"No thanks, Henri, it's all right, your wife didn't count on this."

"Okay, we'll load the plane when you get back."

Henri jerked his thumb at the boy and went inside quickly, he was always moving fast, usually from work to work. Morison walked to one of the town's lesser hotels, really an old, wide, three-story house with barracklike extensions, and settled himself in an eating-and-drinking section which wasn't the hotel dining room. It was like a tavern, all-male, tongue-and-groove walls, beer posters about the Montreal Expos, large round tables with noisy porcelain tops, butts on the floor which was cleaned perpetually by a short silent old man who spoke only at night after a day's drinking. He ordered the steak dinner and two draft beers, something he wouldn't do in Montreal, at least not in a working-man's tavern, and gave the waiter a dollar for the sweeper.

He sipped and then drank from one of the glasses, placed it back on the table with a definite air of contentment, though the Bell's would've been better, and told himself that he was here in real country at last. A cigarette, another good swallow, a relaxed look around the tavern, yeah, this is it. But his mind wouldn't let go, it seemed to insist on things. He felt it forming a

16

query, a doubt, what is this *it?*—a sort of gentle pressure from reality, as if desire stood still briefly and could be seen, a frozen frame in an already familiar replay. He emptied the glass and watched the slipping foam and reached for the next one. He looked around again to reaffirm his contentment. Yes, he said to himself with emphatically clear meaning, I want this.

Then he knew that the meaning was negative, the clarity due to being away: he simply couldn't be doing this with his fellow executives. He could drink with them, they all drank, but with their social faces on, always in work roles even at play, using their personalities as instruments in getting and keeping position or authority or power, always alert for advantage, constantly simulating genuineness the way people once had to feign moral goodness, the real persons submerged perhaps forever under a way of life that dictated everything they did, as rigid as an ancient priestly caste. Here he could admit it to himself. In a tavern full of workingmen. They had their own simulations, of course, but they weren't his. Later, when he was back home, he wouldn't be seeing things this way, he'd be conceding he might be wrong.

He drank the beer and signaled for more. The old sweeper, who didn't look at him at all, went to the bar and took the glass that had been put out for him and drained it in one swallow. You drink too much, old man, maybe I should tell you that, as if you didn't know it, maybe we could have a sensitivity session. Yeah, maybe. It's a sophisticated way of faking genuineness, you tell the other guy what you really think of him, always bad, and he tells you, and the ensuing hatred passes off as honesty. But the guys in this room are simple, they'd spot the hatred, and it'd come to fists, not venom choked back and swallowed and distilled into a special kind of smile. If I told you anything, old man, I'd tell you that I like you, I like the way you suffer, yes, suffer, and yes, like, that's something you *don't* know, and it would be something good to know. The urge to speak became very strong, but he had let the dollar say it for him.

His steak came. And a man who had just entered, followed immediately by two more, saw him and went to his table, cheerful with greeting and reunion.

"Hello, Mr. Morison!"

"Gus!"

"You came early this year."

"Yeah. Say, I figured you'd be on the lakes."

"I was. Just got back."

"Well, well, well." He waved them around the table. They pulled up two neighboring chairs and sat down.

Auguste Benoit, Gus, had been Morison's guide for the last three seasons. He was in his forties, medium height, big in chest and shoulders, with a handsome thickening face, greenish eyes, short brown hair, and small hands that looked delicate against the rest of him. It was said that he was part Indian, but he had never spoken about it to Morison. He knew a great deal about a lot of things and was silent about most of them.

The other two looked like hangers-on, not loafers, just men without work, without money. One was fat and balding, in his thirties, and affected a look of innocence. The other was tall, muscular, of any age, with a beetle-browed angular face, weathered, menacing in repose, but he laughed easily and seemed unconcerned about his few remaining brown teeth. There were no introductions.

"Looks like you got a big one going," Gus said, and jerked his thumb toward Tétrault's.

"With three other guys, over to Lac des Grises." He waved four all around to the waiter. "We're gonna make camp and explore the whole lake." It explained why he wasn't using a guide.

"Should be good there. They were getting ten-pounders where I was. Talk about excited, guys jumping in the boat, yelling at me to gaff 'em, their first time."

They all laughed. The waiter set down sixteen glasses of beer. Gus began to reach, a little obviously, for his back pocket, but Morison gestured no and paid the waiter. The other men hadn't moved.

"Drink up."

A few polite sips, then swallows, a more comfortable settling into chairs, and empty glasses began to litter the table.

"I was up near Grises once," said the man with the brown teeth, "about five years ago, in the spring, oh, maybe two weeks after ice-out. Never saw anything like it. We found the stream and they were so thick there we were shooting at 'em, 22's. Couldn't bring 'em all out, too much weight for the plane, and big, the size of your leg." He drained another glass.

"They're not as good to eat when they're that big," the fat man put in.

"They're wily old buggers."

"Fussy eaters."

"One guy had a big gang troll," Gus said, "and they weren't hitting him at all, he was used to fishing where you see forty fifty boats on the lake and the fish are wise to you. 'What the hell am I doing wrong,' he kept saying, and hell, I wasn't gonna tell him, all you get's an argument 'cause these guys like to think they know. So he started giving it to me for taking him there, in a nice way, you know, but he was packed by then, on gin, and I didn't want the guy to go away with no fish. So I said, Mr. Reynolds, lemme see your troll, maybe there's some crap on it, and I took off all that goddam jewelry he had on there and told him these fish aren't fishing-wise yet and it don't take much to get 'em curious, and he said what the hell any way's better than the bad luck he was having. So he tosses the thing over, and pow! in two minutes they start hitting him, and every time he put out they hit him again, and he winds up with maybe ten big ones, happy like a kid. The other guys, they had two other boats, weren't so lucky, they kept the gang trolls on. And that son of a bitch, Reynolds, never told 'em to take 'em off. He kept getting fish and the other guys kept getting mad."

Laughter all around. And more talk. The stories were a contribution to the occasion. No one believed them, or disbelieved them, they were lived in the telling, the content growing to suit the needs of the rhetoric. The test was not fact or veracity but the effect on the audience, in this case Morison. The men had something, a fund of experience, and they shared it with him like a drama, it was his occasion, not because he was paying for it but because he created it. Morison, sensitive always to nuances, didn't himself attempt a story, that would have short-circuited the flow of anecdotes. His to enjoy the telling, and the teller, to acknowledge the underlying expertise, the years of hard experience, to be Mr. Morison, who had learned some of it, and who could be taken in a little. He wasn't a rich man here, he was simply accepted, differences and all, and it made equality superfluous. He knew these men were realists, not the braggarts they seemed to be: on a dangerous trip they would know exactly the sort of load he could carry and how long he could carry it, and they would do the rest. They had no illusions about their way of life, or his, for they knew nothing about his, and they were able, as he was, to ignore or to cross over cultural barriers.

The talk lasted through another quadruple round of beer, and it was nearly two o'clock when Morison made his way back to Henri's. He was still enjoying the rough companionship and the tall stories. He was in no hurry, the schedule was his own will, things would happen when he decided they would. He watched the sky: the weather looked good, a few clouds, perhaps a bank on the horizon, but clear overhead, a westerly wind at ten, no cold streamers in the upper air. The station wagon had been moved over to the pier alongside one of the planes. The boy summoned Henri who rounded up three young men, his eldest son and two friends, and following Morison's preferences they began loading the Cessna with the wagon's contents. As the work progressed with a great deal of conversation, Gus arrived with his two hangers-on and they gawked at the supplies, examined some of the new fishing gear, and made themselves generally helpful. With eight people, for whom this was routine, the job was done without effort. The case of Bell's was lashed in the passenger's seat, it deserved respect. "I'd rather lose the goddam fish." That was from Gus, an oblique reference to the fact that there was liquor around. They walked back to Henri's store. The eldest son drove the wagon proudly for the short distance and put the rest of the frozen food in the freezer. The other people would fly it to the campsite tomorrow with more supplies, extra gas for the Cessna, and two collapsible boats.

At a long table Morison spread out an aeronautical map and gave Henri the equivalent of a flight plan. Lac des Grises was eighty miles away 5° north of due west, he'd be dog-legging twice to pick up natural landmarks, and he'd stay at 2,500 feet.

"That's okay," Henri said, "there's no traffic up there, but I'd go higher if I were you."

"Yeah," Gus said, "you'll see better."

"At three then."

"Or four," said Henri. "You gotta look at those lakes from way up, so you can see the real shape. Side on is no good. If you're high enough up you got lots of time to look and you can also see where the other lakes are."

"And you cut down on the dog-legs," Gus said.

"Yeah, that sounds good. I was going by the map."

"It's no map up there, let me tell you," said Henri, "bush and water, water and bush. You rely on the big lakes. Hell, you see only this much"—he made a circle with his hands over the map—"if you're low. You gotta be able to see *this* much." He widened the circle to show points of reference. "Then as you go you pick up the whole picture."

"I'm convinced," Morison said, laughing at Henri's earnestness. He took the bottle of Scotch from the briefcase and put it on the table. Swiftly glasses appeared, ice, a jug of water, drinks were made, lifted, and downed with praises.

"I'll show you," said Henri, still on the subject. "The scale there is 1:1,000,000. To make the map they take pictures from ten thousand feet and get a scale of 1:50,000, and that's about this small." He put his arms on the map. "Now if you go at five thousand feet, you get this." He narrowed the area with his hands. "And if you want to go at twenty-five hundred, you get *this*." He inverted an unused glass. "And that don't tell you anything except there's trees down there, and by hell, you know that already."

They all laughed and drank.

"All right, I'll fly high, I promise you."

"By jeez," Gus said, holding up his glass, "I'll be flying higher than that, and with no plane neither."

Morison pushed the bottle over to Gus, folded his map with the route uppermost, and put it in his back pocket. Henri gave him an updated weather report, low pressure to the west, a front that would pass to the south of them. Henri, Gus, and the two hangers-on saw Morison to the plane, inspecting everything and acting as if they were going to catapult it physically. Morison put on the bush shirt, it'd be some fifteen degrees cooler at five thousand feet. With a wink Gus tucked the nearly empty bottle under the pilot's seat and closed the door firmly. It was a matter of pride, or policy, the bottle went with the man who owned it. "Don't fish it dry, I might wanna go there sometime." Morison beamed at him and adjusted his sunglasses.

He was ready. Another moment to enjoy. He started the engine, let it warm up, and finally revved it for testing. He signaled to the men holding the plane back and they pushed him off from the dock. Wind westerly, from behind him. As he taxied he did his cockpit check. He wasn't casual about it, even though he knew the plane had been completely serviced. He prided himself on his professional approach. He got to the far end of the lake, turned, pointed himself toward Henri's, and uttered a satisfied "Go!" He gathered speed, pushing mounds of water, and timed his moves to rock the plane gently and climbed onto the steps of the floats. He moved easier now and faster. Imperceptibly he left the water, climbing smoothly, glanced at his waving friends below, and saw the countryside beginning to spread itself out before him.

He was aloft. At 3:22 p.m.

3

When the plane reached 110 m.p.h. he set the throttle
and r.p.m.'s for climbing, and he imagined Gus still on
the dock yelling up instructions and advice. He chuckled at the idea and finally laughed out loud because he
was so pleased with everything. The terrain below him
lost its large detail and shrank until it seemed to stop
shrinking. Fifteen hundred feet. Bush and water, rib-
bons of streams and small rivers. He could still see
Henri's demonstration with the map, you'll have to go
higher, there's only a glassful of country down there.
He let the plane climb. He felt more and more let out,
almost completely released. He sensed that it was a
slightly negative feeling, and for an instant almost
dwelt on what he was being released from. Free is better. Free then. And the feeling was made more positive
by the horizon expanding on all sides, a thing of his
own doing, riding the apex of a huge growing cone of
vision and awareness. What's a mile down there? A

square mile? Some six hundred football fields. I must have a handful of map by now. Twenty-five hundred feet.

He kept climbing, glancing at the instrument panel from time to time, and at three thousand he throttled back and leveled off to cruising speed. Automatically he looked for other aircraft and wondered if Gus could still see him. It was hazy. The new horizon had cloud, but it was far, no problem. He oriented the map to be able to anticipate landmarks and settled back to enjoy his flying. The radio squawked over the noise of the plane.

"Calling Cessna GMG," it said when he took it.

"GMG."

"Everything okay up there?" It was Henri.

"Sure. It's great. I'm at three thousand."

"Just checking. You got a lot of cargo."

"I'm enjoying the scenery."

"Have fun. Out."

He laughed at the idea of their being concerned. Still, it's good to know they're there, all of them good men. He thought of a drink, said no, then said yes, and got the bottle out from under the seat, drank from it and put it back. Not exactly professional, he thought, but what the heck, it was safer up here than in the Chrysler.

Gradually he grew used to the sights, the seemingly stationary horizon, the slowly passing ground to the sides, the sun almost all the way to his left. He checked the air chart. The ground, like the map, was sprinkled with lakes of all shapes, small from the air, a few square miles, big enough if you were fishing on one of them, but tiny compared to Lake Mistassini. It stood out on the map, forty or fifty miles north and east from where he was, and big. It looked like a hundred miles long. He turned in his seat to see if he could spot it on the horizon, but the air was too hazy. It was the only attraction for miles around. He thought about it, and was tempted to detour, but he held his course. The idea came back to him anyway. He had plenty of gas and lots of time. A holiday, dammit, a holiday, you're not flying a commercial schedule, it's time to be a tourist, go over and take a look.

"The scenic route."

Carefully, as though appeasing something, he adjusted his flight lines on the map and plotted a bearing from Mistassini to Lac des Grises. Then he veered northeast, grinning with daring.

The lake came into view in less than twenty minutes. It began in a jigsaw of streams and small lakes and islands and odd-shaped chunks of land, and expanded suddenly into an endless prairie of water. It was even bigger than he imagined. It was at least ten miles wide, going northeast right into the sky, it seemed, with a strip of long islands running up the middle and disappearing in the distance. He looked at it with fascination, and pleasure, and something like a twinge of excitement. Aloud he kept exclaiming, "Will you look at that," and held the plane to the eastern shore as though the whole maneuver were an emergency.

Quickly he established the time, 3:49, his speed, 125, and decided to see how far the lake went by his own calculation. His enthusiasm grew as the lake developed under him. In five minutes he was able to notice another lake taking shape five to ten miles east of Mistassini and running parallel with it. The map called it Lac Albanel. It ran into a cluster of large islands about the time he had covered forty miles, and emerged into a width of five miles. Together the lakes and the land between them made a strip some twenty miles across and pointing almost directly northeast. And still they kept going.

He passed his estimated fifty miles, roughly twenty-four minutes of flying time, and could see no end yet. He enjoyed the contrast between the map and the actual terrain. The map was exact, theoretical, without mystery, but his exploration was full of uncertainty and, yes, he admitted, thrill. And safety. He wasn't Columbus working, he was Spence Morison vacationing. At sixty miles he thought he could make out a northeast limit, and five minutes later, at seventy miles, he actually saw it in the distance. The lakes seemed to end together right across his line of flight. It was 4:27 p.m., thirty-eight minutes of flying. Mistassini was a good eighty miles long. He felt he had really discovered something. Now for the bird's-eye view.

He climbed to five thousand feet and made a long turn, 180° and more to pick up the lakes again, and headed southwest. He looked below for a while, remembering Henri's perspective—it'd be better higher still—somewhat distracted by the noise of the engine—wouldn't it be something in a glider?—laughing as he tried to figure out the area, half a million football fields, impossible to imagine, you have to see it. Reluctantly he finally told himself he had seen enough, and recalculated his course to Lac des Grises, first west, then southwest, and settled in for the flight to the campsite. It had been a good side trip. Time for a drink.

When he straightened after tucking the bottle away he sensed that something was different. The air was cooler and the west was full of dense cloud expanding to overtake the sun. He hadn't paid too much attention to it before, he had been too engrossed in Mistassini. He looked around carefully. Visibility was still good where he was. There was a drop in atmospheric pressure, which would alter his altimeter reading. The west was getting blacker. The hum of the engine varied with the changing air, and the drinks made him insensitive to slight movements of the plane. He became serious, cautious. He knew he was heading into weather. The fun was over. It was time to work.

He assessed himself coldly, with ironic detachment after the idle fun of Mistassini, and made allowances for liquor, age, experience. He did it with deliberation and not without a hint of professional pride. If he had to go by visuals and by feel, the main instrument would be himself. He began with the weather. What was thought to be an almost stationary front had moved rapidly east, and he'd have to see how it behaved. He'd have a series of developing options: continue to Lac des Grises, detour to it if possible, land and wait out the storm, and as a last resort go back to Chibougamau. He stayed on course, watching the darkening horizon, the banks of wind-driven cloud, and eased the throttle back to start losing altitude. The smaller lakes to his left rippled into a change of color. There was wind, strong wind. He began to drift and adjusted for it. And in five minutes he was into more and more turbulence and he knew he'd have to put down and wait. It was a standard procedure with bush pilots. It wasn't even an emergency measure, you just landed, that's all.

By now he was at three thousand feet, staying below the cloud base, alert for any change in wind direction, and searching the countryside for a place to land. The sun was gone, covered with black cloud. Thunder clouds, which meant heavy turbulence. He dismissed the smaller lakes. He'd need one he could approach from any direction. Finally he saw one, to the south-west, some fifteen miles long with interruptions and at least three miles wide. He went down to two thousand feet, estimated the wind as best he could, brought the plane to fifteen hundred feet, and turned to line up with the lake. He put the flaps down and adjusted the throttle to maintain his speed. He eased down to one thousand feet and from there began a long bumpy descent, seeing larger detail and getting more visual perspective. The terrain was hilly, the water choppy, and the wind had become erratic.

He was at two hundred feet when he came over the water, still high enough to maneuver and glad that he had picked a long lake. The landing would be tricky. He watched his speed carefully, he could stall at 60 m.p.h. with the flaps down. At one hundred feet he was in worse turbulence and had to keep making quick adjustments of the steering column. He reduced power, seventy-five feet, the descent seemed faster, the water choppier, white-capped, fifty feet more or less, he couldn't be sure, but he had to commit himself. He throttled against the gusts, feeling his way down to the choppy water. We're doing it, he told himself, everything's under control, 85 m.p.h. to land, throttle on to make power so the floats can drag. It was raining.

And suddenly the gusts shifted and the wind was everywhere. He touched down hard, the wind behind him, he thought, but he was relieved at the reassuring thud of the floats as they struck the water, and he reached out to cut the throttle. He didn't get to do it. Without warning he was jolted forward, heard the floats banging like oil drums, and felt the plane nose down with heartbreaking screeches. Rocks awash under the choppy water. He hadn't seen them. It was like crashing with the Chrysler. The floats are holed! he yelled in his head, and he was still doing things when he struck the instrument panel, dazed, knowing with a strange certainty that he was going to lose consciousness.

4

He heard the wind and rain hissing around the cabin, and water lapping and gurgling, close and loud, as if he were in a bathtub. He could smell gasoline. He was crouched over the stick, still holding it with both hands, somehow unable to sit up. He was, he knew, resting on the instrument panel, not just leaning on it. The outside was reaching him slowly, fact by fact, each one equally important and lingering, none as yet connected with another. The hissing sounded like steam from hot metal. The plane groaned and rocked and kept scraping something. He imagined his feet were soaked. The next fact was that his eyes were open, that he was looking down along his right thigh, and that he was seeing water. He was almost sitting in it. The Scotch bottle floated next to his knee. Everything was tilted forward steeply, and to the right, which kept the cargo from pinning him to the panel. He took it all in as if he were studying it, emotions not yet arising, significance overriding fear, and he told himself it would be better not to shift his weight. By reflex he looked down at his left wrist: 4:55 p.m. He had some four hours of daylight remaining, for what he did not know.

Very carefully he raised his head and turned it from side to side, expecting pain. But there was none. He saw blood on the panel and knew that the left side of his face was bleeding. He ignored it. He flexed his hands, arms, legs, feet in the soggy boots. They moved all right, they didn't hurt. He was fearful of the next isometric. In slow motion he placed his arms on the panel and cautiously tried his back muscles. To his relief he was able to lift himself a little from the panel. Nothing broken. The angle prevented him from getting into a vertical position, and the plane screeched and jerked downward with a loud crunch. It held precariously and swayed in the wind. The water inside rose a few inches and the hissing grew louder.

For the first time, and thinking it strange to be doing it now, he surveyed the outside. No, it's not strange, he heard himself argue, it feels safer inside, and I was right not to move, cause when I do, this whole thing's gonna move too. He was looking out as he debated. He could see water all around and land on either side about a mile away. The engine was almost fully submerged, nose down, steaming. The right wing was under water, its tip impossibly sticking up, broken, probably not yet sheared off. The left wing was bent back and down, almost horizontal, and seemed to provide temporary ballast. He couldn't see the rocks, he could only hear them scraping the plane. The floats were not in sight. There was no more to know. Except fear. A sudden sting of terror, a twitch of brain and heart, urged him to struggle out of the cabin quickly. With a huge intake of breath he held himself in check. It's got to be done easy, easy, and it's gotta be now.

He snapped open the seat belt and made sure it was out of the way. He shifted slowly to his left, waited, and grabbed the door handle without turning his body. Again he waited. The plane seesawed gently. He couldn't be sure if it was caused by his motion or by the wind. He twisted the door handle and began reaching out, opening the door, holding it against the wind. A mistake. It acted like a sail, the plane tipped, and he let it go slamming against the side. Once more he waited. The open doorway caught more wind and the plane made longer seesaws. He moved all the way left, straight-arming the panel and putting a wet boot against the seat that held the case of Scotch. In that position he leaned out and looked over the side. He still couldn't make out the rocks. They had to be there, the plane was resting on something, but the churning water kept reflecting the broken sky.

He drew back in and twisted and raised himself, his right knee on the panel, his left foot on the seat, hands on the top corner of the door frame, and maneuvered slowly until he was standing in the tilted doorway looking down into the moving water. Furiously he tried to assess things. I'll have to clear the plane, the wing can sweep me under, and the rocks won't do me any good even if I could get on them, they'd be slip-

34

pery, don't kid yourself. He didn't move. Even now it was better here than down there. His thoughts became more rapid, cycling the same alternatives, decisions being made and unmade immediately, his fears growing sharper, and he felt the plane slip under his weight. Still he hesitated. And the plane jerked down again with a definite crack. In the instant he knew, without words to think by, and he needed no deciding. He sprang from the doorway, to his right, feet first in case of rocks, and struck the water heavily and kept going, clear of obstructions, and down.

He felt himself pulled by his sodden boots and propelled by his upright position. It was a long descent. And to him it seemed infinite. He didn't struggle. He forced himself not to. He accepted the silence of the water, the cold soaking, the drumming pressure in his head, and concentrated on holding the air clutched in his lungs. He noticed how dark it was and realized he was still wearing his sunglasses, an irony caught in passing. Somehow it gave him hope. He knew against all instinct that he could sink only so far, and that from then on—unless he was too far down—he would begin to rise, slowly. He was fully clad. Everything depended on how fast slow would be. And hurry would be fatal.

When he thought he could trust himself to act calmly against his descent, he stretched out his arms in slow langour like a man yawning in bed. Right after that he placed his legs in a walking stride and held them open. Then with great mental effort he unstiffened his muscles and made sure he was as limp as possible. It felt suicidal, but he became less heavy and he knew he was decelerating without exhausting himself. Twenty feet, he estimated gloomily, maybe more, in a pool diving feet first he could touch bottom easily, fifteen feet, add clothes and boots already soaked and a body tight with fear and you've got depth. And danger. He knew about chest compressibility and that despite the air in his lungs he could keep going down. The deceleration continued, and in a while he began to feel buoyant. He wondered how long he'd been down, but time was the pressure in his chest, soon to be measured by pain, not a calculation at all but an urgent cry to go up.

He brought his arms to his sides, palms down, and at the same time tried to close his legs like scissors. The boots made it difficult and his clothing held its inertia. He tried to verify that he'd moved, but he couldn't be sure. He might be idling in one spot. Grimly he saw the possibility of nightmare panic, and admitted it in an effort to hold it off. He paused deliberately. If he was going up, he was going up still; if not, he had to save his strength. He tried the stroke again, heavily and uncertainly. Again he paused, this time aware of his vertical position, his chest turning into pain, and suddenly he knew something: he'd be more buoyant flat out. With willed slow motion he maneuvered himself into a face-down position, his legs of necessity dangling, and decided on faith that this was his final course. He made long maximized strokes and rested between them and knew now that he was going up.

The pain was unbearable, but he had to hold onto it like a life preserver.

Gradually the water brightened as if it was preparing a climax to his pain, and he was seeing light and he knew there was more and more to see. He floated to the surface, felt the chilling air blowing on his hair, and as he raised his head, ready to scream for breath, he sank back again in new despair. He had come out too fast and merely bobbed back in. He tore off the sunglasses unheedful of where they went and began a grim pantomime for timing his first intake of air. He couldn't afford to swim normally, he was waterlogged and it would take too much effort. But ironically he was at the surface, all he had to do was float his head out. He let himself glide into an upright posture, and carefully watching the light he repeated his earlier stroke, this time caressing the water softly. As he inched toward the brightness, he committed himself. He blew air from his nose, straining not to go up too fast, cut off his exhalation, broke water imperceptibly, and at long last gulped air into his open mouth.

He rested, as limp as possible, leaning forward, dangling like a rag doll, still hurting but glad almost to giggling for that one breath. He slipped under a little, not far, and not fast, and in a short while he tested his buoyancy. By gently pressing the water he rose easily, but when he raised his head out of it, followed unavoidably by neck and shoulders, he sank quickly, inertia taking him further than he wanted. He was buoyant as long as he was actually and fully in the water;

out of it the real weight of any exposed parts would keep driving him under. He made another decision on faith, you stay up by staying down, an enforced trust in the very thing that could kill him. Ignoring his ambiguous fears he slipped into a vertical position, let his head peer slowly over the top, exhaling, rose to chin level, took a breath and slipped back in. It worked. His relief was like a sigh. Again he rested a little and began to repeat the cycle. He did it perhaps another ten times—he wasn't counting—until his motions and rhythm were one delicate act of breathing. For a time it was all he was doing: staying afloat just under the surface and working and waiting for the next intake of air. But there was more to be done.

In the next cycle he started to orient himself. He was facing south looking along the length of the lake. Underwater, he turned left slightly and came up looking east. He tried to estimate how far the shore was. Another turn showed him the northern length of the water, and another the western shore, difficult to see because of the rain, its distance impossible to estimate. He completed one more cycle and took one more look, north. The plane was not in sight. Nor, from his angle, any flotsam. He wondered quickly, clinging to a hope, if it would be seen from the air when the lake was calm. The idea was a new pain, an unresolved fear, and it felt like an added weight. He took it along, he had to. He chose the eastern shore.

It was a mile away or more, a mass of green bush rising from the water, and it seemed even farther now that he had chosen it. He couldn't swim that distance, even unclad. He'd be exhausted in a hundred yards. And his clothes were becoming a deadly impediment, their inertia prevented underwater swimming. But he wanted to keep them, he'd chill more rapidly without them, and they would be needed later, if there was to be a later. He told himself to stop thinking of the distant shore, he was in water, under it, looking at it and through it, save for the one or two seconds of surfacing. His only recourse was to try to move through it, to float himself toward that shore. He'd have to do it between breaths, and slowly. After his next intake of air, as he slipped below the surface, he snaked his arms before him, leaned forward, strode open his legs, and made a long slow stroke and let himself glide, not far, and lazily regained his vertical position. He eased up for air and rested.

He had no idea how far he'd come: his body's length almost certainly, maybe twice that, say, twelve feet, no, that's too much, ten feet then, in how long, I dunno, count it, thousand-and-one, thousand-and-two, why count it, it doesn't matter anyway. He breathed and tried it all again. He didn't count. He was creating a new rhythm, to move submerged when he had air and to breathe before he really had to. Horizontally he was more buoyant and moved a little more easily, but he had to be vertical to surface without sinking. He tried it again, and again, thinking about it as he rested. Each phase was entire, the breathing, submerging, going flat out, returning to vertical, resting, breathing again. None of it could be eliminated, each had its own time and manner, and there could be no hurrying. Slow moves, rests, a minimum of physical work. It became boring with repetition. Fears dissolved in the monotony. You can't go faster than the speed of water.

Length by length he advanced, living mainly underwater, feeling at times that the periodic wind on his head and face was distinctly unnatural. His pattern of action was absolute, an end in itself, no varying, no straying, no gawking. It wasn't like walking idly, free to look around, to deviate, to think of something or nothing, or even to stop completely. The pattern had to be maintained, it made him breathe and move ahead, no more, and only purpose and destination made it tolerable. There was nothing to see, nothing to tell him he was progressing. At every cycle he saw the thickening opacity of the water below him, no passing objects, no changing perspective, then a brief glimpse of the sky, the shore line, the roughened waters. It was always the same. The shore was as far as the sky.

As the monotony deepened he was twice suddenly tempted to speak aloud, to simply babble his predicament into the water. It would have been a free act, natural and unfettered, environing himself with human sounds, it seemed, asserting his essential wholeness. He both wondered and laughed inwardly at the urge, but he understood its significance. And for a few cycles he dwelt on the question, what would I say? like a shy housewife who might have to go on TV. It was comical in the engulfing water, a lightening of spirit that made him feel more buoyant, and for a moment he feared he might be getting giddy from not breathing right. No, he estimated, I'm getting enough air, the thing is really funny. Detachedly he saw that the care he had taken to examine the joke made it all the funnier, but he had passed the point of humor, he had become careful again. He concentrated on keeping things dull.

He put himself through uncounted cycles. His motions grew more and more automatic, and his mind began to buzz with random activity, mostly worry. The cold he was beginning to feel told him a long time had passed. His leg muscles started to cramp. He wanted to throw off the languid movements, to be able to move faster, to be rid once and for all of this engulfment. He almost raged at it, uselessly, for he knew the slow rhythm would continue, it was basic, a breathing reflex, as fundamental as the return of hunger. He saw himself scrambling to shore, desperate to escape the waters, fleeing from disasters in a haste that was itself disastrous, surprised by sudden agonies and struggling powerlessly against odds as vast as oceans. The images had force and reality, like night dreams. They affected his breathing and made him tense and threatened his very means of surviving.

For something different to do he stopped his advance at the next intake of air and tried to rest passively in the rag-doll posture. But he was too waterlogged, he started to sink away from the light. He held back his fright and slowly waved himself back up, took a breath of air as if it were a rarity, and resumed his advance. The struggle was mental now, and much more hazardous. Outside the imposed calmness of his floating, there was only fear and danger and hopelessness, an environment of panic, waiting for him to lose heart and abandon his discipline. He found it impossible to think in any sequence or plan with any logic, these required a desk and an office. He couldn't even distract himself. The only thing to do was react, to cut off the fear as it arose, shake away the images before they grew, prepare a huge "No!" to hold off the ultimate threat, the real possibility of dying. Seen and faced that way, the fears retreated a little. He imagined them as a physical enemy going back down to the depths to lurk. And again he wanted to say something about it. He was back to himself. But this time it wasn't funny.

For the next long while he wasn't sure he would not panic. The dread of it was part of his efforts, lessening only with his tiring vigilance. As it faded gradually, he felt more keenly the pains in his legs, the increasing coldness in his whole body, the energy lost in mental strain. Things could not get better, the critical path was downward. He knew there would have to be a new crisis, and in hopeless resignation he tried to be ready for it. He took to concentrating on the outside, remembering the sky as he submerged, picturing it as he drifted and anticipating his next glimpse. It was then that he noticed the shore in discernible perspective. It was close.

At the next look he saw high ground, hills, full of trees. And at the one after that, knowing that he was some ten feet nearer and sensing the impact of that fact, he looked for and saw individual trees. They were clear enough to be identified. Each impatient unhurried cycle showed him more and more and always those ten feet closer. He saw the undergrowth, a strewage of rocks, a scraggly beach line. He tried to estimate how far he was. It was too hard over water and at eye level. Under and along and out again. I'm close, he told himself, better than that I'm closer. The monotonous cycles were prolonged excitements. He had to force himself not to hurry. Look by look he edged toward shore, and suddenly, with a surprise that almost made him gasp, for he wasn't looking for it, he saw bottom.

It was clear and rocky and still deep. The shore forgotten for the moment, he watched it slope upwards slowly, rocks diminishing into gravel, cycle by cycle, weeds appearing, more gravel, a fish moving like a touched nerve. He felt his buoyancy dropping off and when he straightened to go up for air his feet touched solid ground. He moved ahead a little and stood, head out, breathing freely and rocking with the heaving water. He was about fifty feet from shore.

He pushed himself toward it with a sort of breast stroke, walking heavily and clumsily in the water, and as he emerged his wet clothes dragged him down. He was surprised they weighed so much. When the water was waist high he could hardly move his legs. He stopped to rest, still relishing his breathing. He didn't want to exhaust himself, he'd be coping with a lot more. He didn't even look around. Slowly he hauled his anchored feet ahead, one at a time, like a man on stilts, and when the water was low enough he used his hands to lift his legs forward. At ankle depth he sat on the bottom and laboriously untied his boots and re-moved them. It took a long time. Then he walked to dry shore carrying them and knelt soggily on the grav-el, looking out over the lake. The wind began to chill him. It was better than being in the water. He stared at the miles before him.

"You made it."

The sounds of his speaking made him very much alive, and alone.

5

The sky was vast, and it seemed to be made of wind. To the west it was full of big white clouds, the warming sun still a few hours high. The south was dark, weathery, and the long waters of the lake were broken into cold grays. He could see the other shore clearly, two, perhaps three miles away. But he couldn't see the plane. He searched through the wide angle of the possible lines of his travel. Nothing. It was submerged, or sunk to the bottom. He stood up for a better view. All he saw was the white-capped water.

He found it hard to look away from where he had been. The plane had carried all his immediate needs and more. It summarized his resources and skills and plans, his status, the capacity to be and do, as though it were his very self. And in a way it was. He kept looking, and wishing, merely wishing, despite his knowing otherwise, incapable of not expecting some technique, even akin to magic, to restore things or to offer some way of doing it.

"You're wasting time."

His voice was like another person's, outside him, suddenly surprising. It said things he wasn't thinking of, things he really knew, and it pierced the numbness of his feelings. It was a strange act of speech, done without internal preparation, an utterance, a babble. Yeah, time, he responded, what time? His wet clothes were getting colder.

"No. Not time. Sun. You're wasting sun."

Yeah, you're right. Automatically he looked at his watch. Waterproof, dustproof, shockproof, but moisture had condensed under the glass. 6:32. I'm gonna need this. For what he did not know, it was like an amulet.

"You have to get dry. And warm."

Unwillingly he looked around him. The shore was mainly gravel, rock-strewn, sandy in parts, interspersed with bigger rocks and boulders and dotted with short tough plants. It went inland about forty feet into a heavy undergrowth beyond which was a maze of trees and bush. He recognized the evergreens, but only in general, and what he imagined to be maples. The rest were just trees swaying noiselessly in the wind and growing taller as they climbed uphill. Their foliage was fresh with every shade of green, bright in the slanting sun, an effect not unnoticed by him, but the mass of it looked impenetrable and full of menace.

He surveyed it without feeling, as if it didn't involve him, so much unusable real estate, a bad place for a campsite, all the while aware that his emotions hadn't caught up with what he really knew. He had survived the water and that seemed to be enough. But it wouldn't do for long. He felt a slight trembling in his legs, an omen of panic belying his seeming apathy, wet socks and feet on stones, and he wondered if it would grow. He knew all there was to know about his situation, he couldn't miss it, but he also knew there was going to be more to it than that.

"Get dry."

He began with his boots. He took them to a boulder about the size of a car trunk, loosened the laces, removed the felt inner soles, put these on the warm rock, and lined up the boots so that their tops were facing the wind. He tried to remove a sock by standing on one foot, but it wouldn't slide off. He had to sit down and pry it off, then the other. It was difficult and tiring, and he gave up the idea of squeezing them dry. He shook the sand from them and placed them near the felt soles. It all seemed so silly. Why not just go inside and change? Simple. Just like that. Go on inside. Yeah, and change.

He worked off the sunglass case from his blackened and soggy leather belt and put it and the belt on the rock. Before doing anything else he decided to empty his pockets. He had to tug things out: a leather key case, coins, some of which he left in the pocket, a butane lighter, a penknife, a thick folded wallet that oozed water when he squeezed it, a hanky which he waved open in a tangled way and put on the rock under the edge of one boot, from his woolen shirt a pack of heavy wet cigarettes, a short bottle opener, the folded and now mushed check list, from his light shirt the receipt from the motel, a gasoline slip, a ball-point, a small brown comb. He let the things drop at his feet, sophisticated artifacts, not yet junk, on gravel as ancient as the moon. He was very conscious of his bare feet.

Leaning on the rock, he struggled out of his clinging pants. In careful steps he walked toward the underbrush, swung the pants in a circle to get rid of the excess water, and draped them over the bushes. He did the same with his woolen shirt, his light one, then the T-shirt. It was strangely tiring. He slid his boxer shorts to his feet, stepped out of them, and spread them alongside the other clothes. He was naked. The wind chilled him, as did the growing realization of things. His hair was still dripping at the back. Shelter. An inside to go to. He was stripped of everything now, except his watch. It showed itself to him automatically, arm bending in a gesture of civilization, 7:04, as though he were waiting to catch a train, or, worse irony, a plane.

"It's five minutes after seven."

He didn't know why he said it. The tone of his voice was flat and factual, as if he were keeping a log or getting close to a deadline. But the very saying of the words was reassuring, he was telling time, speaking it, counting something, it's five after, it hasn't been long, it won't be long, something is going to happen, time is what makes things happen—yeah, but maybe not this time, and maybe not here. It was irrelevant. He felt farcical standing there naked and clinging to his watch.

He slipped it off his wrist and began to pick his way

toward the rock that held his boots. His nakedness made him cautious and apprehensive, fearful of falling, of cutting his feet on the stones, forcing him to make each step a special act of balancing. He stopped, both feet not uncomfortably set, and put the watch back on. He cleared a space around him and knelt on one knee. From that position he cleared more space, advanced a little, and cleared yet more. Touching the stones and the sand made them less of a nuisance, and having dirt sticking to his knees, legs, hands, and feet made him less careful for his naked body. Avoiding pain and cuts made sense, but trying to avoid dirt or even mere contact was a civilized taboo, a dangerous one. Dirt wouldn't bother a kid.

"He wouldn't have 180 pounds of pressure on a heel bone either."

And he got his own message. Deliberately and with dignity and some effort he sat down on the cleared area and put his arms on his knees. The ground was warm. There was less wind. And he thought he could feel the sun's heat.

"You're wasting time."

He looked toward the sun, which was now closer to the horizon, got up, brushed the dirt from his buttocks and testicles, and moved toward the rock again. This time he did it in short paces, without the balancing act, placing his feet one by one where they told him he could press. A technique had replaced fearfulness. On a flat rock near the one holding his boots he put the watch down on its side, facing the sun. But he had lost the reason for doing so. Why am I doing this? It's silly.

I want to dry it out, the rock's warm. Your body's warm, it'll dry out on your wrist. Well, it's safer here, I don't want to break it, I might fall, and the rock's warmer than my body, I can feel it.

"Check the time when the sun goes down."

And again when it's dark. That'll tell you how much twilight you'll have tomorrow. Dark. When it's dark I won't be able to see it. Check it before dark. And then? Then . . .

The fact of approaching darkness made him feel helpless and suddenly weak. He felt it in his legs and arms, a quivering held down by a strange heaviness as though fright was competing with despair. He realized that despite his conscious actions he had been thinking of this place as a makeshift campsite and that he had not acknowledged its grim prospects. He'd have to cope with the night, do more than lie naked on the gravel, make sure that he kept or regained strength and do that by finding some kind of shelter and some kind of food. Food? Here?! It's only till tomorrow. They'll find me. They're good men. They're sure to find me. Panic wasn't far away. And illusions of security could lead right to it. He knew he'd have to do something, and now, while there was light. He was beginning to feel his nakedness inside.

He took his wet boots from the rock, used them as a scraper to clear a space in the gravel, sat down, slipped them on his feet and tied them by winding the laces around his ankles. They flopped a little without the inner soles and squished as he put weight on them, but he was less helpless now, though no less farcical. He made his way to the water's edge, staying on dry land, went to his left, going south along the shore, and without searching for anything in particular looked for whatever he could see.

The beach stretched in front of him for about a mile and ended against a hill of vegetation and rock. He decided not to go that far. He walked slowly, carefully, pausing every few steps to see things from each new angle of vision. When he had gone about a hundred feet the brush to his left became sparse and formed an opening into the bush behind it. He went as far as the edge of the clearing and stopped to look past it like a man peering into a doorway. Walking through bush, he knew from experience, could tear clothing, let alone exposed flesh. And without clothes he couldn't push his way past boughs and twigs and small trees. What he saw was a woods not too heavily overgrown, passable in places, a maze of trees, some black and leafless, hardened by death, a few hollow with rot, others fallen in tangles, and most of them pushing long high trunks skyward, fighting for the sun. He groped his way in, virtually on tiptoe.

He noticed the coolness and the drop in the wind, and almost immediately he heard and felt the mosquitoes. Ironically, the woods were no shelter, he'd have to spend the night on the beach, in the open where the wind would keep the insects away. He thought of the tents that had gone down, the insect repellent, the clothes, the camp stove, the lost food that would still be good days from now, weeks even. And the tools. The knives. The hatchet. Well, they're gone, that's all there is to it, there's nothing. A low moment, the chill of despair: his hands felt as naked as his groin.

"Come off it, they'll be here tomorrow."

Maybe. You better assume they won't be. Think it out. They've got to get to Lac des Grises first and—

"Think it out later, you'll have all night."

Without shelter. He moved a little farther into the woods, not quite knowing what he was going to do. There was deadwood everywhere. A lot of it was on the ground, partly hidden by small green plants, but it was heavy and rotting and of no use. There was some in almost every tree, except the evergreens, wedged or dangling or hooked precariously ready to drop off in the next strong wind. Some of it had fallen upright and leaned against the trunks as though protecting them from further damage. Limbs from dead trees had snapped, but not free, and made a dry and brittle contact with the earth. The ground was covered with short fresh growth and twigs and small branches and layers of leaves, the mulch of years, blackened and slowly composting, the debris of uncounted winters. No campsite here, not without tools and a whole technology behind them and time made especially into holidays. Nature doesn't recognize holidays.

He tugged at a hanging branch suspended just above his head, a long thing like a small tree, and jerked and twisted until it fell with a crackle of breaking twigs. The big end, about five inches thick, bounced up and scraped his right leg, not seriously, but it was enough in these circumstances to make the task demoralizing.

He dragged the branch to the clearing and heaved it onto the gravel beach. Another mistake. He was already tired, and the intense brief effort winded him and made him feel suddenly weak. He went back into the woods, slowly, found another branch leaning on a trunk, took it down carefully and, making no attempt to lift it, he pulled it behind him as he walked and finally placed it on the beach next to the first one. He paused, rested, and went back into the woods. Trip by trip, with enforced calmness, expending as little energy as possible, he laid out over a dozen branches.

The work left him sweating and short of breath, surprised and shaken by his fatigue, for he had fancied himself in better condition. He stopped awhile, trying to do nothing, chilling once again, and itching with swollen mosquito bites, none fortunately in his private parts. But all he could do was look at the inhospitable beach, the loose row of deadwood, his clothes on rocks and bushes some hundred feet away. The sun was getting red, cooler, not an hour away from the horizon. It all felt silly, futile, grimly comical, without promise of relief. Better to keep working.

One by one he dragged the branches to his original site. A hundred feet one way, leaving a trail behind him, a hundred feet back, slowly, restfully, the process repeated in measured monotony, basic human labor, until the lot had all been moved. Again one by one he trimmed them of their twigs and smaller limbs, making a pile of these and passing up anything that did not break easily under hand or foot. When he was finished he had in effect a jumble of long crude logs or thick poles, varying from ten to twenty feet, three to five inches round, with smaller branches sticking out all over. The longer ones he broke into shorter lengths by hooking them under one rock and snapping them downward over another. In one operation he had firewood and building material, a nice stroke of automation.

The sun was gone now, leaving strips of shining red cloud around half the horizon. The west was a glaring blue that somehow managed to seem cold. He had to look at it. It had a significance for him, a new one, a frightening beauty, remote, indifferent, not the made-up aesthetics of sunset at camp. He felt he was peering at it through a small unaided self. He had lost the sun. 93×10^6 miles away and moving. A device for getting tanned, floodlight for a golf course, the definition of a nice day. He could claim no rights here, make no complaints. The small self. He was afraid.

In the new twilight he went back to work. He took one of the longer and straighter pieces and placed it along the top of the bushes next to his clothes. It swayed and wiggled on the small thick branches, and he jammed it down and made sure it would at least stay in place. On the adjoining ground he cleared the gravel of stones and smoothed it out as well as he could. He had and vetoed the idea of trying to collect sand for bedding. With the ground prepared, he went back to the supply of wood, picked out suitable pieces, brought them singly to the cleared site, and finally positioned them one end on the gravel, the other leaning against the crosspiece on the bushes until he had a makeshift lean-to long enough to cover him. Over it he put an uneven layer of bigger twigs and smaller branches, and over that he laid all his clothes, except the hanky and his belt, hoping to make his contrivance more of a windbreak. He didn't crawl into it to test it, there was nothing he could do to improve it, he had to accept it as it was, for now. Shelter, at least a psychological shelter.

"I need fire."

He spoke it musingly to the blackening lake, the shore line that was losing color, the amorphous forest. The diminishing twilight told him to be quiet, not to reveal his presence to the impending darkness. In daylight he'd be somewhere, localized, bounded, in a known range, but in the dark he'd be everywhere, spread out, a sensor, knowing things only by their suddenness, too late. I still need fire.

He knew the odds were against it, but he kept working anyway. He gathered the tiniest twigs, some thinner than matchsticks, and ground them against his palms to get some sort of tinder. Between the lean-to and a big rock some twenty feet away in line with the wind he built up a pile of fuel, the tinder, twigs, small branches, bigger ones, and finally the crude logs peaking upward in the middle. It would blaze fast and hot and could be banked to burn all night. Nearby he stacked more logs in case they'd be needed. It was all set. By habit, and realizing it as soon as he moved, his hand all but touched his thigh, feeling for a pants pocket that wasn't there.

From the scattered pile of his personal belongings

he fished out the butane lighter. And he knew, of course: he snapped it and nothing happened, only the gas hissed out. The flint was still wet. He blew on it a few times, but didn't try it again for fear of losing gas. He placed it on the rock with his belt and hanky, something he should have done hours ago, remembered his watch, took that from the neighboring rock and put it on his wrist. 9:07. He had forgotten to check the time at sundown. It bothered him not to be dressed, not to have his things in his pockets. He gathered them in the hanky, all but the lighter, which he left, and the belt and sunglass case, which he carried by clutching around the hanky, and took them to the lean-to. He emptied the wallet and spread out the paper at the base of the bushes, the business cards, the money in fifties and twenties and tens, fives, ones, old memos, license, registration, passes, all soggy. He dumped out the credit cards and wedged the wallet open with a stub of wood. The cigarette pack and the check list were too mushy to pry apart, the gasoline slip and the motel receipt he hooked on the bush. The hard objects he cached well inside the lean-to as though hiding them, the sunglass case, the penknife, the bottle opener, the comb, the key case. On impulse he took the belt, straightened up, and buckled it on so that it rested on his hips. A good place for it. Wet and cold, but not for long. It meant something, it was heavy and sturdy, an inch and a half wide, it bestowed a feeling of strength. There wasn't the slightest hint of it being funny. He was girt.

There was nothing left to do now but wait for the

dark. The woods were becoming denser and deeper, green sinking into black, the lean-to signaled by the white T-shirt and the less white drawers. They should be dry soon, sooner than the other clothes. The gravel was disappearing into a gray flatness that could have been a highway except for the boulders and rocks, which now looked more distant, smaller, softer. The wind had dropped to being a firm breeze and the lake glistened and rippled, gentle as only water can be, in front of the still clear west and the silhouetted tree line of the farther shore. For the first time he saw birds darting against the sky, and thought he heard them, but the breeze and the water absorbed their sounds. Open country, beautiful and menacing. And he was still naked, very white and very visible, except for a pair of boots and a belt and a watch.

He made his way toward the lighter on the rock, sweeping a path with his boots as he went. The scraping, scuffling noises he made surrounded him completely, as loud as a rockslide, and he imagined they could be heard for miles. The noise made him deaf to other sounds, cut off from the outside, vulnerable, without alert or warning, susceptible to any suddenness which could be made known to him only by being upon him, by touching, by contacting his exposed body. Fear. For the moment fear was an environment. And it would stay as long as he was making noise. And he kept doing it. He felt as he had when he was deciding to stay underwater. Deliberately he maintained the environing clatter, accepted the fears which grew no less, and completed the simple task of clearing away a few stones as he went to his lighter. It was either that or spend the night immobilized by terror.

The lighter was large and chromed and brighter than the rock. It was invested with emotion, too much emotion, and meaning. He was learning a hard lesson. The first thing he should have done on reaching shore was to dry the lighter, to foresee such an elemental need, remove the flint, place it on the warm rock, enshrine it, carefully protect it, and now be able to use it. A waterproof container of matches, in case of soakings by rain or fishing accidents, at worst an inconvenience, was stowed with all the carefully planned equipment—in the plane. He snapped the lighter open, and quickly shut. No spark. He couldn't remember which way the gas-jet control should go, so he left it alone.

He went back along the scraped path, the gravel crunching under his boots, stopped at the prepared wood, squatted, and began to blow on the lighter's wheel and flint. It became a rhythm, a periodic hiss in the descending darkness, a lulling forlorn sound. In the stillness he began to feel his hunger. It was an urgent signal accustomed to immediate response, and it was all the stronger since he knew he had no food. The alcohol was wearing off, leaving him tense and jumpy. He couldn't smoke. The quiet time for thinking had been an illusion. He couldn't be quiet inside. Hunger brought fear with it, and both would grow.

He kept blowing on the lighter, disheartened, close to tears, shivering with dread and the chilling nightfall, aware.

"God, I wish I had a drink."

6

By 10:40 it was dark. And it seemed to be as dark as it would get. His eyes had grown used to the night very gradually, changing as imperceptibly as the slowly fading light, so that the moment of darkness could not be defined. The hands and numbers of his watch glowed clearly, he had forgotten the dial was il-luminated, it didn't matter, it only confirmed that it was night.

To his relief he found that he could see. He had ex-pected to be enclosed in blindness, alert with hearing and nerve ends but not with sight. The night was not total blindness, and it wasn't enclosing. He saw shapes and was able to know them, a peak of opacity next to him that was the readied firewood, the much lighter ground under him traveling all about designating the beach, the huge interruptions of dark rock fused with the gravel, an infinitely extended sheen that was the lake, bright by contrast, catching his peripheral vision like insistent taps on the shoulder, behind him the absolutely dense forest, the invisible lean-to marked off by the floating white T-shirt near the black entrance. And above him an intensifying mass of stars that made light-years seem close. The only details were the stars. The rest were vague though definite presences at uncertain distances and of undetectable substance. His own hands lacked lines and boundaries. But he saw. He saw enough to feel himself defined, a common center of wholeness, a chilling body, sensitive to environment, and itchy, hands to grope with and touch, the final orientation, ears centralizing a sphere of sounds, unscrambling a jumble of noises, how near, how far, how strong, all somehow made reassuring by a vision however diminished, and his interior self, somewhat newly present and strangely evident, from which could emanate fear, and hope.

He kept blowing on the lighter, easily, with long pauses, careful not to hyperventilate. He needed a fire to get heat. But with a fire going, he would hear less. And with it would also be light. And with light, ironically, he would see less. He kept pondering the thing, as though it had a philosophical importance, chill, firewood, vision, one as factual as the other, fire, light, heat, realities ready to cancel realities. If he had a fire he would see the fire and little else, it takes a lot of light to be able to see everything, light so strong you can't look at it. And hot. So it has to be far away. It *is* far away. I've just discovered the sun. He blew on the lighter as though he were laughing and looked at the negatively silvered water. Not looking, gazing, presenting a gaze, wide-pupiled, peripheral, not a speck of color, the set's on the fritz, it's gone black and white, I was in there, in the water, four hours ago, no five hours ago, four hours ago I started drying out, drying the stuff, that is, yeah, face it, it was both. How much had I had? Not much, just a few beers at lunch, one for the road. Nothing serious. Nothing at all. Four hours. Some of that stuff must be pretty near dry.

He got up, stiff from squatting and kneeling, and saw that he had moved into a new perspective, higher off the ground, things dimmer, the lake more insistent, new blacknesses to guess at. It was a sort of disorientation, and it made walking difficult. He waited, unfocused wide-open eyes staring at the gravel between himself and the lean-to, the T-shirt irritatingly clear in his side vision and all but invisible when he looked straight at it. In a short while he stopped trying to see his way, and deliberately not relying on his eyes he let his legs move forward, stumbling slightly when he touched ground before he expected it.

He bumped softly into the entrance of the lean-to, shaking the whole structure and causing the bushes to rustle. The T-shirt was hardly damp, dry enough to wear. He still had the lighter in his left hand. Not wanting to risk losing it, he placed it carefully between his feet, put on the T-shirt, which made the rest of his nakedness feel absurd, groped for the shorts, dry except for the waistband, and had the problem of putting these on over his boots. He sat down and managed it, always conscious of the whereabouts of the lighter, and stood up to brush the dirt from his backside and to fit them on properly. With the lighter back in his left hand he felt the rest of the clothes, all very damp still, decided against trying to sleep just yet, and made his way back to the firewood.

He felt better with some clothes on. They were significant, closer to normal, like beachwear or something for a back-yard barbecue, no guests, maybe friends, close friends, but no ten-inch boots and no belt against the skin, why not, maybe the belt, a weekend hippie. Barbecue. The great outdoors of suburbia, nature as dining room, and bar. Consumers. Closer to normal. What normal? He squatted, blew on the lighter, and cautiously tried it. Click, click. Nothing. Uncomfortable, he switched to kneeling on one knee, still uncomfortable. He groped around in a crouch, made out a likely flat rock, confirmed by hand, not too heavy, and pushed it along into position next to the firewood. He sat on it and continued blowing on the lighter. They'll find me.

The idea began a speculation that was largely worry, a quiet time for panic. He tried not to think, but that felt like a mistake, another lack of foresight, the blunder of not facing things, a card unturned that might have done the trick. What trick? Of course, they'll find me. No. That *may* be true, but it's not accurate. What's accurate? They'll search for me, that's what. The rest depends. It depends. He broke off the argument and looked at the southern sky, deep with stars. Something definite to look at. Engage the senses, bypass the mind for a while. The long swing east of the Milky Way, the galaxy edge-on. Where am I? North always there, a balancing act of relativity, forever more or less, spaceship earth, they say, locked on a blank space near Polaris, a self-support system without computers, only they don't say that, it doesn't fit the diagram, or the hologram, a tiny tidy earth, until you look at it, the sacred cow is a lot of bull. Only man can know. And what does that mean? Something, just something, it seems to be a key. He heard and then listened to the noises from the forest: chirps, trills, rolling squeaks, all separate and all regular, they made a pulsating entirety, one reinforcing the other in a continuous high-frequency gurgling, a sort of statistical siren. Like crickets, or early summer frogs. It left other sounds quite audible, a snapping twig, a scufflelike shaking of leaves, short soft groans, a briefly warbled hoot, distant cawings, the odd quick fluttering, and from the lake only an occasional swishing of water and the imagined audibility of the weakening breeze. It didn't scare him in any way. Perhaps it was because he had no weapons. He went back to work. Click, click, nothing.

He could see them circling Lac des Grises, examining the north shore for the agreed-upon clearing, and wondering why they couldn't see anything. Three of them, and their pilot. Good friends. Martin, a doctor, a heart specialist, thin and tough, with curling gray hair, always hankering for a cigarette, so he said, though he quit years ago, a good diagnostician; Eric, the youngest of the group, computer expert, anything can be programmed, who'd laugh as the matter got more absurd, but in a humorless way like someone from another culture, and begin to plot the options against the contingencies; and Gerry, a lawyer with the company, a big ponderous man who spoke slowly from having everything already done in his head, achievement being only a matter of persistence, sooner or later things respond to organization, and so would this. They'd fly the perimeter of the lake once and take a good look, then land and go to the clearing and check and recheck to see if I got there at all, and find nothing, no plane, no camp, no supplies, no Spence Morison. End of holiday, no need to spell it out, red alert, emergency. They'd never let it lie. They'd radio in immediately, directly or by relay, and start flying back on a parallel course, in dog-legs if they had the fuel. It won't do any good, with that storm coming up I wasn't on that course. From Chibougamau the search'll fan out and they'll find me. If the fan's big enough. And if I can signal, or make a marker, smoke of course, and a fire. More clicks in the dark, more nothing.

The scenario put him into tomorrow, a whole day's events, hours upon hours of tense and boring work scanning the bush, seeing and not seeing things, he making efforts here to direct the vision in his head along lines that led to him, all of it peopled by these friends, by Henri and his brothers, in full daylight, with the sound and smell of planes, the hopeful straining search. A long tiring time went by, in a few seconds. And the scene, unsustainable, was replaced by reality. They'll be phoning Betty, probably Martin, he knows her the best, and she'll break it to Nancy and Tom. Oh God, the worry, the disruption, just when they think I'm on a holiday. No, Martin wouldn't phone right away, he'd wait until it was . . . until. The thought refused to complete itself. There are things you should never admit, even as a hypothesis, so don't. The fan will be big enough. It'll have to reach at least a hundred miles north of anything they're going to think of. That's big, maybe too big.

He stood up to interrupt the fearful thinking, but the anxiety remained. It was built into the situation. Only the damfoolest of boy scouts would be optimistic, no, not scouts, they're just kids, scoutmasters, nature conquered by virtue, the smile as a badge of happiness, another illusion, another comedy. So what have you got against scoutmasters? Nothing, nothing at all, except that I'm here, not prepared, that's all, which makes them right, but not all right, nobody likes to concede anything to the other guy's virtue, to his skills maybe, and to his luck for sure, but not . . . His mind ran on with indiscriminate debate, overactive, hyper. He had to urinate again. The pissing late-forties. Yeah, that and the booze. How much did I . . . ? He groped his way past the surplus branches and into their tracks going south, the known route, form-bound. Not in the lake, that might have to be my drinking water. At a short distance he went toward the bushes, chose a likely rock and relieved himself against it to cut down the noise. He couldn't see anything, no change of tone, no black spot forming. Some of it splashed him a little, it didn't matter, the function was comforting. Then a stab of hunger, and trembling muscles, sharp, weakening hunger. He knew he had to ignore it as best he could or it would become obsessive. He inched back to the waiting firewood and actually had to find it close-up before he was sure he was in the right place. He sat on the rock again and concentrated on the design of the lighter.

He couldn't really see it. All he could do was make it out, a tone less deep than his hand which in turn was less deep than the ground. Had it been a new and unfamiliar object, he couldn't have known what it was by trying to look at it. Memory and his fingers did the work of his eyes, hard smooth chrome, slightly etched, tiny screws, the striking mechanism, the gas-jet control, the large screwheads for filling it and changing flints, the brand name and patent information running like a puzzle along the bottom. He couldn't remember the brand name. He knew all this was there, he could actually see it in his mind and, differently, feel it with his fingers. The two sets of knowledge remained apart, un-unified, independent, and yet now the hand was realer than the eye. He pictured a diagram of the channel that contained the flint, the spring, and the holding screw. It told him very little except that the channel could still be full of trapped water. It should be taken apart and dried. Of course. In the dark. A flint dropped on a gravel beach. A tiny spring flying loose into the darkness. Might as well throw the lighter into the bush. Maybe undoing the screw just to see if there *is* water in the channel. To see? You can't see! Take a coin . . . From where? From my right hand pocket. You mean, go to all the trouble of going over there and digging out a coin from a pair of wet pants? . . . take a coin, loosen the screw a little, and find out. You won't

66

find out anything, you won't be able to feel the water, it's no tap, you know, just a drop of water spreading out over the cold smooth chrome. He pictured what would be happening, if seen, in the dark, and abandoned the idea. It was replaced swiftly by another one: the striking wheel is probably clogged. And refuted just as fast: how can it be clogged? I've only tried it a few times.

Without further argument or even thought, he snapped the lighter open, quickly put his forefinger over the gas jet, and kept working the mechanism in abbreviated snaps and blowing on the unseen and partly exposed striking wheel. He hoped that this would shave the wet flint onto the file-toothed wheel and hasten the drying by evaporation and friction. It engaged him fully. He brought everything to bear on this recalcitrant piece of metal, stiffening posture, all muscles peaking to his fingers, hands and head close as if he were sniffing the problem, eyes imagining that he saw, ears ready for the crisp rasp of dry flint, all for something he'd toss in the garbage at home and replace with ease, with money, something you wouldn't even bother to repair, or, more truly, to get repaired, again with money. It presumed a high order of technology, an environment full of it, service, instant fire for a cigarette, all you have to do is puff. It was meant to be replaced, not salvaged, a throwaway, cheaper to get a new one, a toy to smoke with, fire was obsolete. At moments he felt ludicrous, a boy once more worrying a piece of junk. Timeless. Strangely patient. There was only this to do. Don't waste the flint. Wait.

He closed down the lighter and waited. More ideas and more pictures came to him, mainly from his fingers. Rub two sticks together. "Ha!" And something moved, fast, in the woods. He ignored it. How not to? Clean the wheel. Thumb under the lighter at the front, forefinger over the gas jet, the middle finger could then prop the thing open all the way, all with one hand, the left. He tried it, it worked. He felt for a small twig, found one about the thickness of an old-fashioned wooden match, broke it to get a stiff and hopefully ragged end, and set about propping the lighter open and scraping the wheel. He worked at it, blowing away imagined flint dust, until he thought he had done the full circumference. He disengaged his fingers, put the twig between his boots, and tried the lighter. Nothing. He did it twice more, still nothing. On the fourth try it caught and flamed.

He had fire.

He didn't do anything for a moment, he was trembling with excitement, and enjoying it. He took in the darkness with relished suspense. He could do something about it now. Easy will do it, easy. Everything had been, and still was, a crisis, a series of them, big and small, from getting away from the plane, floating to shore, to struggling to get his socks off, making a shelter, scrounging firewood. He felt as if he was getting away with something, not guiltily, but surreptitiously, as tense as a thief, almost giddy with pilfered liberties. He could claim no rights here, everything was a gift, or a theft. Coming up now was heat, and dryness, and light.

On one knee, not heeding the sharp stones, he felt for the prepared tinder and understood that it was too low for the lighter, he'd have to direct the flame downward with a strong jet and that would waste fuel. With one hand he picked up a small bundle of tiny twigs, dry and brittle, held it shakily as low as possible, brought the lighter to it and clicked it on. The twigs caught immediately, like a miniature torch, as good as holding a dozen matches together. In the new light everything was different, accessible. He held them at the base of the pile, branches visible and dancing with shadows, and waited till the kindling was well caught before letting his starting bundle fall apart and disappear into the warming flames. In a minute all was ablaze except the heavier peaked pieces. It was going to be a huge fire. I'll keep it going till they find me. His watch said 11:45.

7

He had to keep moving back from the fire. It wasn't cozy, it was too intense. It was a mass of noisy flaming heat, sometimes ten feet high, roaring and fluttering as it settled slowly over a super-heated white core. It was as beyond his control as his circumstances, and it disturbed him. Sudden, frightful, consuming—the way, he imagined, panic would be. The change had been too swift, from the quiet enveloping darkness, the patient clicks of the lighter, to this—a burst of light and heat and noise. Too much. It had altered his carefully perceived environment. The surrounding night was deeper and closer, the sky invisible to unshielded eyes, the outer sounds unheard over the gushing fire, rocks and beach temporarily new, unstable in the nervous light. You don't adapt to fire, at least not to a big one. He stared at it, fixed, with unwelcome excitement. A waste of wood. But there was no cutting it smaller, even if he had an ax he couldn't afford the energy, or the time. Time. Anyway there was lots of wood, and lots of forest, and the branches needn't be stacked in a peak, they could be slipped in from the sides.

He dragged away the flat rock, now warm, sat on it and pulled off his boots and laid them out to dry. It was good to be warming himself, but strangely it wasn't pleasurable, not the taken-for-granted relaxation into comfort. Camping is comfortable, it means not losing comfort, guys bring air mattresses, foam-rubber pillows, folding canvas chairs on tubular aluminum frames. What do you want on a flat rock, half naked? Nothing. Just the warmth from the fire, and drying out. I'll take it as it comes. He felt the beginnings of disillusion, of hurt, resentment, something dissolving away—a notion about himself and nature, too vague to identify. Involuntarily he kept looking at the jumping flames. Light, and movement. The eye couldn't resist, it took an act of will to look away, and then not for long, like meeting someone's eyes. He respected the fire like a presence: evoked, alive, somewhat to be feared. You couldn't take it for granted, you had to watch it all the time. It wasn't friendly, necessity never is. The luxuries are, though, aren't they? Friendly, familiar, despised, a nuisance after a while. Like a superfluous fireplace that needs cleaning. I wish I could stop thinking.

But he couldn't stop, and he couldn't fight it. He remained squatting on the stone, not moving, tensed as though ready to get up, and for a long time he looked at the fire and listened to it and watched its progress, still resenting its necessity, until finally he became vaguely interested in when the burning logs would slip down. It was a detached interest in some alien thing. The fire didn't feel like his, it felt like someone else's. And his mind leaped instantly to the question: whose? Nobody's, nobody's, he was quick to head off his runaway thinking, just not mine, that's all, not mine. The effort stiffened his body, and he noticed how rigid he had become: legs drawn in, arms pointing forward, his left hand still squeezing the lighter, his chest tight, head and neck locked in grim refusal, all because of an inner turmoil. He tried to dispel it by unclamping his jaw and letting his taut muscles loosen a little. It helped, for a while. But gradually he grew tense again, and noticed it only when he was as rigid as before. This time he stood up, feeling a wave of heat from the fire, it's too hot, I built it wrong, and walked gingerly, barefoot, to the lean-to where he placed the lighter carefully with the rest of his things. It was cool in the lean-to, its slanting logs kept out the heat of the fire, too cool to sleep in unclad. I built that wrong too. He started to walk around it in normal steps and was pulled up short by the gravel hurting his feet. At least there's no glass on the beach. The words were so clear in his mind that he wasn't sure he hadn't spoken them aloud. He almost laughed, tearfully. Nothing was normal.

He inspected his clothes on the lean-to, they weren't dry, they were too far from the fire. Another thing wrong. Despairingly he added up the immediate problems: he'd have to sleep in the open, facing the fire; he'd have to get his clothes dry, near the fire; and the fire itself was too concentrated in a peak, it would need a different arrangement, he'd need maximum heat and slow burning, or at least not the fast burning he had now. He went back to the flat stone, sat down once more, and put his boots on again. In a way he was glad he had the problems, it gave him something to do. This time he looked at the fire differently. It was the key factor in three problems, all related. He'd rebuild it and exploit its energies. It would be less alien that way, more something of his own choosing.

He went to his stockpile of wood and picked out a medium-sized sturdy branch some eight feet long and about as thick as the hitting end of a baseball bat, something he could use as a poker. He brought it to the huge fire and, braving the heat, drove it into the core at the base, shoved the still-peaked logs to his right and quickly moved out of the way. The whole fire collapsed in an explosion of sparks. With the crude poker he spread the core to his right and left and arranged the burning logs in a line over ten feet long and running parallel to the lean-to. He waited a little to see what more needed doing, put his poker aside, and sat down on his rock to see how the reorganized fire would do. It did well. The spread-out core was very hot, the logs still flaming easily. He went to the back of the fire and made the rest of the logs parallel and poked them closer to the front. Again he stood awhile, feeling tired now, and looked around him in the light of the fire as though taking possession of the territory. He went back to his seat and gazed at the result of his work, rested, and planned the next job.

He decided on how to dry his clothes. He returned to

the stockpile and tugged out an unbroken branch, a big one, with limbs forking high over his head. He pulled it, in stages, past the fire and placed it with the thick end toward the lean-to and the branches angled near the fire. He collected his clothes, like laundry, now encouragingly damp, and draped them over the branches, high where they'd get more heat. He was wet with sweat by this time, and weaker. He took off his T-shirt, hung it on the branches, and resumed his seat near the fire and waited. The laundry looked good. So did his fire. One more job to do.

When he had caught his breath and dried out he went to the lean-to, removed the smaller branches he had strewn over it, and began placing each semi-log in a more upright position. He jammed it into the gravel and pushed it against the brush as far as it would go. It was tedious, difficult work, especially this late, but by going slowly he finally completed a sort of slanting wall. If it had once prevented the heat of the fire from getting inside the lean-to, he reasoned, it would now act as a reflector with himself between it and the fire. At the base of it he spread twigs and small branches, not ideal, but they'd provide better cushioning than the gravel, a place to lie down, perhaps a place to sleep. He made no attempt to try it or test it, he knew there was nothing he could do to improve it. It was done. That was it. Leave it alone.

He went slowly to the fire and stood to survey all his work: the long low blaze of normal height like five campfires strung together, the clothes on the branches looking still and tired in the dancing light, the changed lean-to that looked like part of a fort behind which, with his other things, was the lighter. He was anxious to have it in his pocket. Soon, he told himself, soon, things are working. A pain in his bowels made him walk to the lake and to his left, the direction that meant toilet. But he didn't find it funny, it was cold away from the fire and he was still sweating. Do it here. And he did. From even that minor distance the site seemed remote and small, an unprotected glow in the vastness of nature at night. He shivered and went back, watching the site acquire detail and become more real, feeling the not yet painful demands of hunger. He circled it idly, past the fire, between it and the water, around to the makeshift clothes dryer, past that to the lean-to, and back to the fire, he was loath to lie down. It's time to get off your feet. Yeah, yeah, I know, I know. His T-shirt was dry. He took off his boots, broke two branches of the dryer down to size, and slipped the boots over the ends to dry. He put on the T-shirt and tenderly made his way to the lean-to. There he lowered himself to sit on the twigs, which settled under his weight, not yet uncomfortably, and he adjusted his back against the uprights.

It was his first genuine respite. He could feel his body wanting to sag into relief and his tension preventing it from doing so entirely. There was no sighing here and saying this is the life and isn't it great and boy will I ever sleep tonight. It was nothing more than: this is better than standing or squatting on a rock. Positive rest was another matter. His feet on the un-twigged gravel were anomalous, his legs, the shorts, the belt, T-shirt, arms, the watch. He looked at the watch. 1:12 a.m., already tomorrow. I'll know today. Don't kid yourself, with that sightseeing, you were too far off course. You know now.

The argument didn't continue. He felt his exhaustion creeping over him and his spirits darkening with despair. He was looking up, seeing the stars, when he slipped into a doze, clearly conscious that he was frightened.

8

He knew his muscles would ache the next day. It was a knowledge that floated through his head like a bothersome fly, disappearing and returning, unconcentratable for long attention. A hot shower, steam, would have prevented it, he never ached after a workout at the Athletic Association, and a drink, and another, he was in good shape for his late forties, but not for going naked in the woods. He was in the handball court, then the swimming pool, marveling that he was dressed for the court, and also for the pool, special white shorts, running shoes, a sweat shirt, even a glove on his hand just to hit the ball with, then tight-fitting trunks, he looked good, big and heavy, but good, not misshapen, confident, every activity had its own tools and technology, its right dress, its own planned places and spaces, its own time and vocabulary, office, house, eating, sleeping, sport, washing up, sitting around reading—and now he would ache, the knowledge said, because he had nothing but his two hands, and feet, and body, and himself. You don't turn on this thing, it's logs and twigs, and you're not lying down. This isn't the way to do things. We'll need two tents, four sleeping bags, two axes, one small bucksaw, frozen steaks. He spoke into an intercom criticizing the bunglers and ordering the job done over again. Orders. Authority. Say the word, and things happen. You don't do them yourself, the wheels do it. Fix up those muscles. Not this time. He saw naked clothes and wondered how that could be. Was it clothes peopled by nobodies? An abstract. Does the mind dream? The puzzle turned into nothing, lingered as an uneasiness, and faded away completely. He was hearing something moving in the woods, and he awoke easily, unafraid.

It was still dark. The stars had moved, of course, but he hadn't noticed them enough earlier to orient them now. The fire was low. He lay still and listened. The sounds were brief scurries, a short swift passage through the bush, a snapping twig, all irregular. A small animal, a fox, a raccoon, even a squirrel, no matter, he had camped often enough to welcome their presence. It was breezy. He felt chilly and stiff, his muscles would be sore. Slowly he bent one leg, then the other, put one hand behind him and levered himself to sit up. The twigs made a lot of noise. He rubbed his arms and legs, they felt clammy. He was too tired to be tense, a good feeling in its own way. He sat with his arms on his knees and looked dumbly at the glowing coals. Work to do. Yeah, in a minute. He could barely make out his clothes tree.

The woods behind him were now quiet, the coals hissed a little and made dull pops, leaves rustled somewhere, and he thought he could hear the water on the shore. It was a pleasant moment, with memories of having gotten up in the middle of the night to stoke a fire and gone back to a warm sleeping bag. But in the instant he was more fully awake and again aware of his sinister context. He checked for a spot to put his feet, stood up, and felt his way to the fire. He poked at the embers, which flamed out quickly to the other pieces and became a big fire again. He stayed near it to get warm and moved back as it grew more intense. He was grateful for it, for its shape, and its heat, and its light. He wasn't using it for his own pleasure, or wasting it on aesthetics. It was giving him something sorely needed, and it gave it with strange beauty. It was his by gift. The thought kept him looking at it as he edged to the clothes tree. Middle-of-the-night-thinking, it'll be different in the morning.

His clothes were dry. They were slightly damp from the night, and perhaps the thicker parts hadn't dried out fully, but they could be worn. Eagerly he put on the denim pants after shaking sand from each foot, took the belt from around his body, slipped it through the loops, pushed the pockets in place, and rubbed his thighs in appreciation of the protecting denim. He sat down, wiped his feet and pulled his socks on, slipped the felt soles into the boots, put those on, still very damp, and laced them loosely halfway and wound the laces before tying them. He stood up immediately and tried them like a man buying new shoes. Then the light long-sleeved sport shirt, whose buttons he fumbled in his haste and whose touch made him feel warmer, and finally the heavy woolen bush shirt, dearly welcome, which felt like half a blanket. The hanky he shoved in his right back pocket like a crowning touch. He was clad, fully clad. He shuddered with relief, and in his delight he examined his clothes as if he were going on stage to make a speech. A huge crisis had passed. Symbolically he was back to himself. But only symbolically, and he knew it. That past crisis was meaningless, the real ones lay ahead. Still he was warm, and dry in the main, in his own clothes, shielded from mosquitoes and covered against the night, and nothing was going to stop him from enjoying it. He rubbed his woolen arms and hugged himself and looked thoughtfully at the fire. It gave a lot when you start from nothing.

He walked with freer steps to the designated toilet and then back to the lean-to. The lighter he put in one pocket, the right, and the penknife in the other. He didn't touch the other things. He rearranged the twigs so that he had a mound for a crude pillow, looked at the fire again, raised the woolen collar around his neck, and stretched out full-length, this time with a sigh. In spirits not depressed he waited for sleep to return.

He hadn't looked at his watch, and didn't.

9

The morning light awakened him like a voice. It kept beckoning and he kept resisting until he opened his eyes to see what was catching his attention. He had slept deeply and perhaps long. He was on his right side facing the fire, now out except for a trickle of smoke, and he was looking into a broad sky that seemed enormous, universal, for it was all he could see from ground level. The vast day had begun.

He was fully oriented, he knew where he was, no illusions about being in his own bedroom, and he remembered everything. The degree of his clarity surprised him. He didn't dwell on it, he accepted it as part of the situation. He moved arms and legs and confirmed that he was sore all over. Slowly he rolled onto his stomach, got on all fours, careful not to let his muscles go into spasm, and eased himself to his feet. He didn't stretch or jog. The beach was still in shade, the sun behind him over the woods, the waters in front lit by the slanting light, calm and undulating without ripples. It was well past dawn. He checked his watch, it was 8:15. With deliberate care he took it off his wrist and wound it, telling himself to remember that he had done so. And something else told him to make it a habit.

He crooked his arms and moved them like wings and did slow knee bends with his hands on his legs like an old man trying to sit. Satisfied that his soreness wouldn't get worse, he walked around the site just looking, made his way to the water's edge and eventually to the toilet. From there along the shore away from the site, looking, then back toward it. He couldn't think of it as a camp, he wasn't camping. He felt the day's stubble on his face, vacationlike, outdoorsy, and he wished he could shave. His mouth was dry, he was thirsty, hangover-thirsty, and he realized he had lost a lot of liquids urinating and sweating. He wondered about drinking lake water and decided against it. Treat all water as impure, somebody had said at a lecture at the Association, an after-dinner thing about roughing it, even a sparkling brook could have a decaying dead carcass upstream. Yeah. He continued a short way past the site and turned. And as he did so his hunger gripped him like a slow cramp, insistent, urgent, just short of being real pain. It made him irritable, and shaky, and he felt himself oscillating between sharp anger and panic. He was sweating.

It's pyschological, he told himself, I missed supper and I'm missing breakfast, that's all, I'm not starving and I'm not weak, not yet, it's not time for that. Will there be a time? He didn't answer. His legs were trembling. He sat down on one of the bigger rocks. The sun will be here soon and I haven't got a hat. In a while he felt stronger but still wet from the burst of sweating. He took off his heavy shirt and held it over one arm. I worked hard, getting to shore, getting the wood, making this, and the drinking, and I stayed up late, that was a mistake. It was only for one night. You can't be sure. He started to get off the rock but sat back again. He looked out at the lake and tried to take things step by step: he could wander around or just sit, and both meant that he was doing nothing, except that wandering would tire him. He saw that there was the vacuum of having no chores to do, no cleanup, no airing of sleeping bags, no shaving, no fishing gear to get ready, none of the usual camp things, and no food to prepare, no food at all. He didn't want to face that, his mind wouldn't come back to it, and his head even twisted away from it. Just sit. Sit and wait. They'll come. But the assertion lacked conviction. Gradually, as he reviewed his actions, he realized that he had struggled through the evening and most of the night, not for survival, but to hold out until the plane got here. It had been a deep and unshakable assumption, and it was coming to light painfully. Despite all his conscious thinking, he had felt he could endure all this for the time it took the plane to find him. A day. Two days. Three at most. It had been a faith as firm as bigotry.

"You—can't—go—by—that!"

He bit the words toward the gravel and jerked a clenched fist as each one came out. He held his arm tight with emphasis and let the exhortation sink in.

No, I can't. He let his arm drop.

In three days you'd be too weak to wave a hanky. And it might take them a week. A week! They'd give up long before that. No, they wouldn't! Search and Rescue might have to, but the boys wouldn't, they'd spend their holidays looking, they'd hire help. Looking where? The question, though valid, veered subtly away from him, it promised too big an answer.

He looked out on the lake—gorgeous scenery, terrific fishing—and regarded it as a colossal piece of bad luck. He scanned the middle for traces of the plane, for flotsam, perhaps food that could float to shore, white Styrofoam containers, or maybe the light plastic tackle boxes that were guaranteed not to sink, or the rods with long cork handles, the less than half bottle of Scotch, even a sleeping bag, or the map, a hat, or something spottable by a searching plane. There was nothing but his hunger. A raft. Maybe the water's shallow out there. It isn't. He remembered his initial plunge, the going down and down. A raft of what? Dead logs and twigs and gravel? A long search for materials, days to build it, heavy work stoked by heavy meals. Sure. Everything came back to food, it was basic, just as the fire had been last night.

There is no food.

No, that's not true. What's true is that you haven't got any.

Yeah.

He knew he had no choice, he would have to face the wilds. Nothing would happen to help him here except what he could make happen. Anxiety was even more tiring than the physical work, and that doubly lost energy would have to be replaced, day by day, until they came. The idea chilled him with terror and brought him to the edge of defeat.

"You're not gonna sit still for it."

He walked back some thirty-odd feet to the site and stood in the middle of it. He had no reason for going there, it was just a place to start from. He didn't know what to do, and it wasn't time to do things, it was breakfast time. He couldn't prepare for anything, no ax to pick up, no sheath knife to slip on his belt, no map to consult. It was like doing nothing and having to have it turn into something. He wasn't even at a real place.

He fumbled in his shirt pocket for cigarettes until he remembered where he'd put them. No wonder I'm jumpy, I haven't had a smoke since takeoff. But he sensed that was a weak explanation. He took an impulsive step for the lean-to and stopped. Later, he told himself, later, they're probably still wet anyway, and you can dry them out at high noon, there's something else to be done first.

Without thinking further about it, he went south along the beach, carrying his wool shirt, past the toilet, past the place where he had gathered wood. He went very slowly in a sort of enforced leisure. The thing could not be hurried. South, not north, south was where he should be, and so far whenever he left the site he had always headed in that direction. The mind at work, and heart, an instinct. He grunted in mild amazement. It was a sign of something, maybe a good sign.

He followed the strip of beach for about a quarter mile, ambling and looking at nothing he could recognize. He couldn't see the site from here. He made a mental note to put up a marker. He set the time. In the bush you go by time, not miles. It was 8:30. Less than a mile away was the rocky point with short trees on it. He scanned the bush from there to where he stood, looking for a clearing, and could see none. He was too low and too close, he'd have to be on the lake to spot something, or in a plane. He didn't know what he expected to find. He felt that a clearing would have more growth, a greater variety of vegetation. He continued for what he thought was another quarter mile, halfway from the point to the site, and decided to cut into the bush. He'd be going roughly east. To come out he'd go west. He couldn't get lost unless the sun disappeared. Lost from what? He was already lost. Lost from a lot of hard work he couldn't do over again without asking for serious trouble. He set the time again. Close to 8:40.

He went in. It was much the same as yesterday's section. There were lots of evergreens, some birch, and others that were just trees to him. The undergrowth was heavy, the floor was old leaves and fallen wood, springy and rotting. And it was cool, damp, and full of mosquitoes. He put on the wool shirt and raised the collar. He made his way forward, careful not to trip, not to step on slippery mossy wood, avoiding thick clusters and low-hanging branches. His path became an intricate meander tending east. He could see flashes of sun quite often. It was slow work. He kept at it step by step with the air of a man climbing over a barbed-wire fence. He stayed within his breathing limits, not sweating, trying to idle his way in that one direction. He wasn't going anywhere. After what seemed like a long time, he began to go uphill, gradually getting into less dense bush, less dampness, more sunlight. The footing was better, but he had to work harder. He stopped when he began to get too warm, leaned against a tree, and decided to sit on one of its big roots. It was five after nine, about a half hour into the bush. He probably hadn't gone more than two hundred yards. It felt like two hundred miles. He was tired, and thirsty, and hungry in persistent cycles of growing pain. He fought off a wave of self-pity, but he couldn't fight off his discouragement.

There was food here, he knew, but he didn't know it to see. Dandelions he'd recognize, lawn weeds with a yellow flower, and poison ivy, to keep away from. You could live off the country, some people have gone into the wilderness and lived well. But you started with a cabin, and you brought in food supplies and had a good rifle to hunt with, and you stayed in touch with somebody somewhere. Nobody did it with nothing willingly, it was pointless, it would take a great deal of experience, and if you had that much experience you'd know enough not to try it.

He was looking absently at the trees about him, from one to the other over and over again, and suddenly, when he noticed them, they looked almost familiar, free of threat or menace. They were trees, not just trees, but *trees,* solid, alive, patient, they had a right to be there, they weren't in the way, unless you tried to go through them. The whole forest was present to him. That's another good sign, maybe.

"What did you expect to find, a restaurant?"

I might've at that.

"Come on, let's go."

He continued meandering east. He found he was doing it with less effort now, less subjective strain. He took time to look at things and began to see more than firewood and obstacles. He noticed new growth on the ground and on the trees, moss, fungus, mushrooms which he wouldn't try, ferns, a small brown squirrel chattering from a branch, a hole that he thought was a woodchuck's, the clumsy flutter of a heavy bird, some kind of partridge. The woods seemed to get thinner, with less stubby evergreens, but more grasses and more pines and other trees with long trunks. In a while it became parklike and flat, and he thought he had reached the plateau of the hill. It was 9:30. Time for another rest.

He was an hour from camp. No, not camp, the site. Camp is where you have the necessities: the utensils, stashed food, a tent, and the rest of it, and you have to go back there to eat and sleep. All his necessities he had with him, his clothes, the lighter, the small penknife. And the watch, yes. He wondered why he was attaching such importance to the watch. It was as if time wouldn't be real without it. Certainly place wasn't real without a camp, anywhere is nowhere, any place is no place at all. He felt the ground, which surprisingly wasn't damp, and sat down slowly. His muscles hurt a lot less. Immediately he made a decision:

I'll go south from here, on the right, then cut back toward the lake. Or try to. He wanted to get up again and get going, but he forced himself to rest for ten minutes, by the watch. I don't have to go back there, I can camp anywhere. But if the lake is still they might be able to see the plane underwater, if it's not nose down, or too deep, and I'd better be near it, that's the first rule.

"That's a lot of if's," he muttered.

There isn't a thing that's not an if.

"Except this"—he looked at the woods—"and me."

When time was up, he made his way south by keeping the glinting sun roughly to his left. The plateau seemed to rise a little, more as an elaborate mound than a hill. There were more bushy top-to-bottom evergreens grouped in clusters that looked impenetrable except on all fours, birches of all sizes, and short twiglike growth on the floor. Some of the birches had been gouged or ripped a few feet off the ground, probably by falling branches. He stopped at one point and sniffed at the scented air. It cheered him somehow, it was like a sort of welcome that had not been withheld. He was about to, but didn't, scoff at the idea.

"It's not your fault," he said to what was around him, and he didn't think it strange. "It's mine." And he walked away from the place.

He pressed ahead, taking crude bearings from time to time. The terrain grew flat again, and in a short while it began to slope downhill. He saw more scraped birches and expected to see fallen branches, but there were none around. He glanced for them as he kept moving, routinely watching his footing and immediate passage, and glanced again as he sensed the problem, and finally stopped and looked with curiosity. Something had made those gouges and scrapes. He went over to the birches and examined them. The scrapings were mainly horizontal, not sharp or clean cut, the bark torn across and left hanging, as though a hand had grabbed the tree and torn it. And then, of course, he knew. Jaws. Animal jaws. It was so simple he laughed. All right, what kind of animal? And he laughed again, he didn't know and couldn't. But with that he knew something else.

"Birch bark."

It was an old cliché of outdoor talk, Indian canoes and forgotten long-ago lore, an ancient technology now a mere word, part of the junk in handicraft shops. But it wasn't junk here, it was food, animal food.

He tried to remember what he'd heard and perhaps read about survival, but it wasn't there. He had always half heeded these things secure in the belief that he'd have all the equipment and communications he needed to meet any emergency. And the brains to use them. Stay with your plane. Build a shelter early. Rest. Ration your food. An emergency kit contains fishing line, matches in a waterproof container, a signaling mirror . . . it was all so organized, it presumed you had these things, or some of them. He took out the three-inch penknife and opened the larger two and a half-inch blade. It felt about as adequate as a toothpick.

He made two cuts vertically about a foot long and a few inches apart. He made another cut across the top and began digging and loosening the strip as close to the wood as possible. When he had a long enough flap hanging from the tree he looked at it carefully. Between the bark and where the wood had been there was a relatively soft pulpy material, whitish and stringy. He scraped some of it off with the knife and put it in his mouth. At first it was just foreign matter, chewable, with a taste like sweet sap. He kept chewing it until it lost its strangeness, but he couldn't bring himself to swallow it. He spat it out and tried another, and still couldn't swallow it. It was too unnatural. It was like getting on all fours and eating grass.

It was worse than that. He felt that if he swallowed it, he couldn't hold it down. Or if he did hold it down, he'd be sick in some way, now, or later. His revulsion was total. But he didn't want to give up. He compromised by scraping together a fairly large wad, chewing it, swallowing only the juices, and spitting out the pulp. He was fearful of even that much, but he had to start somewhere. Angrily he determined to continue. He cut out another piece of bark, made another cud, chewed it, swallowed the liquid, spat out the rest. It seemed to quench his thirst. He did it once more. It can't kill you, it's just birch tissue. I don't want that stuff in my stomach. Anyway, I've got enough to see what'll happen.

Nothing'll happen, you'll see.

He moved back from the tree, staring in frustration at the peeled bark. He was shocked by his irrational refusal to eat. Nothing's going to happen, the pulp's edible, it's food. The fact did no good, he acknowledged it fully and still could not bring himself to act on it. He closed the knife slowly and put it in his pocket. Some other time. With feigned decisiveness he looked for the sun through the branches and continued his way south.

The incident stayed with him. He remained upset over it, unable to calm down, saddened, almost shamed by it. He did little more than just keep moving ahead, step by step, avoiding obstacles, not trying to notice things or look for them. He found the going more difficult subjectively, fearing that his foraging might come to nothing. Something more to worry about, and there may be more yet. Gradually, over what seemed a long time, his emotions faded and the episode lost its vividness. What was left was the memory of failure, a dangerous failure. His first serious encounter with nature. He didn't have time to brood over it. He noticed a sunlit area a little distance ahead, a clearing. He zigzagged to make sure by seeing it from different angles. It was there all right, and it grew as he approached it.

At the edge of the clearing what he noticed first was the heat. It was damp and oppressive, the hot air unmoving against the cool of the forest and thick with mosquitoes and horseflies, he thought, and flittering bugs of every variety. The air buzzed with them. He walked ahead quickly to avoid them, and found it noticeably cooler with a slight breeze coming from the right, lakeside. He stopped to look, and told himself with misgivings that he had found his clearing.

It spread out on all sides forming a shallow valley perhaps a half mile across, uneven with hillocks and depressions, tending in general down toward the lake and rising all around to come to an end against more forest. What made it a clearing was that it had no trees. But it was far from clear. It seemed in the overall view to be made up entirely of short bushes, waist-high, spotted in bunches, scattered among tall grasses of all kinds, wildflowers, leaf plants in profusion, the whole forming a jigsaw pattern of paths and varying greens. He was surprised at the dottings of color, white blossoms, yellow flowers, variegated patches, swaying islands of light orange tops, blues, sharp reds, all sprayed about at random. Across the middle of the valley was a strip of higher growth, a thick dense green, as tall as trees and running in the direction of the lake. He didn't know what it meant, but he noted it as characteristic of the valley, a landmark.

He had imagined that finding a clearing would be some sort of answer, that he'd see things he'd recognize, a plant like one in his wife's garden, or some kind of fruit, berries maybe, or even something like what the supermarkets carried. But what he saw was a new problem, a thick lush mass of a thousand species offering no information at all. He strolled into it at a loss, wondering how to minimize his disadvantages.

The sun seemed hot for early morning, and high. He looked at the time, it was twenty to eleven. He took off his heavy shirt, and tried to be more at ease, but he felt his hunger come back sharply like a fearful reminder. Slowly, with no haste possible, he began to dawdle his way across the clearing, in stops and starts and deviations to get a better look at things. Nothing he saw gave him appetite. It wasn't a job for his eyes, he'd need some kind of system, a rough criterion to narrow down his choices.

It's a job for your mouth, he reasoned, dismayed by the very words, you'll have to taste everything, a taste can't hurt you. He decided to hunt for young greens, test them for tenderness, veto anything that had an unpleasant or strong taste. Not exactly scientific, but it cut down on the chaos. Even at that it was hard to zero in on a specific plant. He did it anyway, in a crouch. He took a leaf near the bottom of a plant and tried it. It was harsh. He tried another plant, it was tough. The next one tasted a little like mint. The crouching was awkward and tiring. He sat down next to the plant, pulled more leaves off and munched them. He felt like someone in a Charlie Chaplin movie. They were tender, pleasant, mild. They passed the test, but that didn't really mean anything. He didn't eat them. He tasted the similar neighboring plants, not trusting to his eyes for verification, broke them off near the ground, stood up and stored them inside his light shirt at the waist. Another compromise. At least he'd have them when things started to get unbearable. By then, he knew, it might be too late.

He continued his browsing and his testing. He tied the heavy shirt around his belt by the sleeves to be free to work with his two hands. He kept bunches of one plant that grew low to the ground, had a fan-out of leaves like bigger and rounded dandelion leaves, and tasted mild and crisp though not all that tender. He made allowance for its being raw. He'd never be able to cook it anyway. As the work went on, he became less squeamish about chewing greens and less self-conscious about testing them. With that he became newly aware of his storing them in his shirt. And he realized that he was presuming there'd be a time and a place to eat. There wouldn't be, there wasn't. The idea gave him pause. He sensed his attitude changing like a drop in temperature, and he looked afresh at the crowded field.

"This," he said with an insistent finality, "this is all the restaurant you're going to get, right here."

So I'd better pay the bill, he retorted, there's no use stalling. His next test was a two-foot plant with tiny yellow flowers at its top. He snipped off part of a leaf and put it in his mouth. It wasn't enough to taste. He took more and chewed. It had a flavor he couldn't pin down, not harsh, like some sort of wild seasoning. It was tender, but he chewed it a great deal anyway. Raw greens were supposed to be hard on your stomach. He resigned himself to swallowing it and did so without debating the matter.

He took more leaves and ate them, and parts of the stalk, the yellow flowers and their stems, and finally pulled up the plant, tore off the roots, and finished the rest—the equivalent, he estimated, of a small side dish of salad. He expected to be sick later on. It would be smart, he decided, to eat only the one species, so that if it had bad effects he'd know where they came from. One species, eaten slowly, chewed well, and not all at once like meals, but spaced out over the day. He browsed for the next while, picking and storing the yellow-flowered plants, and finally ate another one. It would take an enormous amount to replace his lost energy. If one plant was ten calories, he'd need two hundred plants a day to keep up a minimum of strength, four hundred if he worked hard. He'd be getting a great deal of cellulose roughage, no protein, no fats, no sugars except maybe the nectar in the flowers, but some flowers contain powerful drugs, and some are poisonous. These yellow things seem all right, anyway you'll know in a few hours, for sure by tomorrow, and by then I may be out of here.

When he felt he'd crammed enough in his shirt, he began to explore for other things, not searching, for he knew only too well that he wasn't equipped to find anything. He kept seeing his familiar plants, the original something-like-mint, the distorted dandelion, the yellow things. On a bush he saw berries, still green, on another red ones. Vaguely he remembered there was some kind of rule about red berries, they'd known it as kids, too far back to recall. He picked one and squeezed it. It had no pit, just tiny seeds. A rule somewhere, deep down, and way back. It would have to stay there. He returned to his foraging until he grew tired of it, almost bored even by his own needs. It was intense work, slow, frustrated by his ignorance, and very low on yield. He decided it was enough.

His watch said a little after 11:15. It was much hotter. He had crossed close to half of the valley and was approaching its middle strip of green growth. He thought he heard the wind grow stronger, but he didn't feel it, only the same quiet breeze nudging the colors in the field. But the sound persisted. It was a sort of rushing rumble, too generalized for a plane, but he thought of it, his heart jumping to the alert at the very idea. He stopped to listen. It was like something in his ears, but he knew it was objective. As he kept walking, the sound grew stronger and clearer, and suddenly, before it could take shape, he realized it was coming from the heavy green growth. Water. Flowing water. It explained the growth.

He pushed into the border of heavy bushes, past another wall of heat, and entered a less dense corridor of scattered small trees, quite penetrable, cool enough to be chilly, and filled with the noise of tumbling water. Some twenty feet in was the brook. The water rushed along a shallow stony bottom, impeded by rocks of all sizes which seemed to grow larger and more numerous upstream. The banks had varying declivities, steep in most places, but not high, almost flat in others, revealing here and there a thin layer of topsoil from which clung tough twig-like bushes. The channel, where he stood, was some fifteen feet wide, and the water covered about half of it. It wasn't deep, a foot at most, and it ran fast over gravel that had been washed and eroded for centuries. The water sparkled where the latticed sunlight broke through, and darkened and disappeared into the shadows downstream.

He couldn't help admiring it for a moment. It was a surprise, a discovery, and he felt quaintly possessive about it as if his knowledge had joined him to it. He now knew it to be there, knew where it was, and knew also that it couldn't be moved away. He attached a great importance to it, as he had to the fire, and the food. It would be a relief to have a way of finding out if the water was drinkable. A big relief. He shrugged it off as impossible and began walking downstream along the dry upper bed. The problem went with him, flowing at his feet on the left. He thought of going upstream to look for the hypothetical decaying carcass, a long hard trudge for miles over rocky ground, and it would prove nothing unless he did find a dead animal. The fatigue involved was probably as bad as being sick. He'd have to do it by trial and error. By drinking it, and waiting. But not now. He had a long way to go to the lake.

He figured he had traveled two sides of a rectangle, one east, the other south, and was now on the third side, the west, which was equal to his first lap. A rough guess put it at four hundred yards. There was no hurry. He felt tired in a sleepy way, though not weak. He was still nervously hungry but without the urgent irritability he had had earlier. And he was thirsty in a gnawing dry way that came from his whole body. The water bothered him like a nightmare stranger who was deciding what to do with him.

The stream wasn't consistent, and before long he had to leave the upper bed and detour into the trees. The water narrowed into a gorge of boulders and splashed its way between them. It came out spraying and foaming, and in a short while spilled into a deep pool and eased out over a long flat. He followed it patiently and took to resting with it when it ran smooth. It kept snaking and changing, always over rocks and stones and pebbles, until at length it took a straighter and more uniform course. It widened and leveled out, more gravel appearing in the bottom, then silt. The bush on the sides grew thicker and closed in on the banks and finally forced him to step into the stream. He saw fish scurry away, too fast to tell what kind, and he thought of all the fishing equipment in the plane and the holiday attitudes that went with it. The association was made in a flash before he knew it, and it was gone as swiftly. Only then did he think of the fish as food. And he had nothing to catch them with.

He waded through the water into the tunnellike overgrowth. Ahead he could see strong sunlight. Another clearing. But it wasn't. As he came out of the overhang he was looking at the lake. It was too soon to be there, he hadn't gone the four hundred yards of his earlier estimate, he must have miscalculated his traverse. But he felt sure he hadn't, he'd gone with the sun. He checked his watch, 11:45, three hours in the bush. Of course. In that time the sun had moved 45° south, and by following it he had traveled in a rough triangle which put him close to the lake. It made him feel better to know. Being off course held too many ironies.

The brook ended at the lake in patches of vegetation by simply blending into it. There were no little falls, no babbling, no delta, just the channel and an underwater current that would attract fish. To the south along the shore the clearing he had just left continued in a rough way for a half mile and became forest again. To the north, on his right, and quite close was the rocky point and beyond that, a mile away, was the site. He enjoyed a brief satisfaction at knowing where he was, relatively. But what was foremost on his mind, more urgent than his half-assuaged hunger, was a burning worrisome thirst.

He undid the wool shirt from around his belt, laid it out on the stubby vegetation, and into it put the greens he had accumulated in the shirt he was wearing. He rolled up the whole thing and jammed it under bushes in the shade near the mouth of the brook. Unencumbered he stepped into the water and went back upstream past the overhanging brush, past the darting fish, the silt which now churned as he walked, and stopped where the bottom was clear and stony and the water flowed swiftly through the rocks. He stood and looked at it. There was no test for this, however arbitrary, and only one choice. The water was clear, fast-moving, aerated by splashing over dozens of barriers, and filtered by a mile and more of stones and pebbles and washed gravel. It could still be trouble. He scooped some in one hand and put it to his mouth. It was cold, of course, and tasted good, a touch of minerals, the faint savor, sometimes imagined, of outdoor water. He didn't expect it to taste otherwise. There was no criterion, no data, just the water with its external purity, and his need. It was unimaginable that it could contain a virulent poison. Some sort of chemicals maybe, a purgative that would give you the runs and weaken you and dehydrate you. Was it sulfur that did that? Memories of springtime, and childhood, and a grandmother who had lived on a farm all her life and who insisted on cleaning everybody out come sugaring time. What was it she used? It was irrelevant, but he'd much rather have that as a problem. Time to stop thinking.

He squatted in the shallow water, facing upstream, ladled it with cupped hands, and drank it slurpily. He did it seven or eight times, spilling a lot, until he figured he had taken about a cupful. He felt a lot better, for now.

Immediately, without hurrying, he went downstream and out of the brook, retrieved his wrapped greens, and walked along the beach to the rocky point to see if he could get by it lakeside. The beach narrowed around it but didn't drop off. He passed easily without having to wade, and on the other side he looked at the long shore and saw nothing he knew. He wasn't tense anymore, only heavily tired, and alone. He had taken his chances, and the next few digestive hours would tell. It was turning out to be a long walk. He was over a mile from the site, and he felt infinitely far from home.

10

It took him over a half hour to reach the site. He simply got there, a placed marked by ashes, some makeshift firewood, the foreshortened lean-to. He felt no sense of arrival, of being glad to be back, it was just a matter of having returned to a starting point. He was relieved that the morning was over. The day and the time pressed him for attention. It was Saturday, the day of the rendezvous at Lac des Grises, and twenty-five to one, which meant, if they were on schedule, that they'd been flying from Montreal since noon, the first lap of what they thought was a holiday. He put his shirt-wrapped greens in the shade and decided to check his bearings with the midday sun. To prepare for this he took a branch that would be relatively straight in silhouette, around an inch by three feet, and shaved one end to a point. With a rock he hammered it into the gravel, keeping it as perpendicular as he could and turning it to present an even side to the sun. He smoothed the ground where its shadow lay, got another branch ready, and waited.

It was hot on the beach. The effort of pounding the stake left him sweaty. His head itched in many places, a pronounced heavy itch as though something had settled there. When he felt his scalp he encountered bumps that broke and got sticky as he touched them. Quickly he looked at his fingertips. They were covered with brownish blood. He felt all the places in his hair, the hairline, his neck, temples. The bumps all bled as he rubbed them, and they all renewed their itching. The bleeding bites meant black flies, a real hazard in the north. Stories were told of lost men so bitten they went out of their minds. Stories. It was hard to keep from scratching. He went to the water's edge and cleaned his hands, and decided against washing his hair, it'd be better to let scabs form. It was something more to worry about, and he accepted it unemotionally as part of the circumstances.

The heat reminded him of his postponed decision to dry his cigarettes. He got them from outside the lean-to where he had placed all the soggy materials, a flat pack of twenty-five, and took them to the beach near the sun marker. The pack was deformed and still damp, and he had to slide it open carefully. He placed the outer cardboard sleeve in the sun, slipped out the two foil sections, put the inner wrapping with its mate, and peeled away the foil. The cigarettes were still soaked, discolored, swollen out of shape, and the bottom layer dripped with leached juices. They were too wet to spread on the sand. He made a crude flat layer of small stones and on it placed the cigarettes one by one. Three of the filters broke off. All told he had twenty-one. It didn't seem worth it, working on a hot beach, using up energy he could ill afford, to salvage something that would normally be flushed down a toilet and replaced right away, by the carton. But these couldn't be replaced, and a smoke would be welcome, dirty brown and all. The filters were still white, they seemed to justify the salvage. He went back to his waiting.

At 1 p.m. EDT by his watch, hoping it was still accurate, he planted the second stick into the north shadow of the first and hammered it into the ground. It was now high noon. And he had a meridian, somewhere near the seventy-fifth, an inch of shadow about two feet long running north-south, with two markers to capture the instant. The lake, he noted, tended west of south. The knowledge didn't change anything, but it gave him the illusion of control. He could now be more precise about where to look.

He stayed till the shadows separated, and walked away looking for shade. But the only shade was in the bush along with the black flies. He'd need a high clearing with a few trees and a wind blowing. A hat would help, of course, but he didn't have one, and contriving one with his shirt would be too cumbersome. He went to the lean-to, pushed aside the twigs he'd slept on, pulled the logs back one by one to their original angle, and put the twigs on top of them. It made plenty of shade. Using his pack of greens as a pillow, he stretched out on the sand inside the lean-to and felt how tired he was.

He knew he couldn't sleep, and wouldn't even try to. He was waiting out the heat, and the time. And as the time went by, his waiting became more anxious. Over and over again he imagined the air route from Montreal to Chibougamau, 290 miles, cruising speed 150 m.p.h., a chartered four-seater, another Cessna unless there'd been a change in plans, two hours to Henri's, they'd be in high spirits, doing a little drinking, anticipating the first catch of fish before supper, the first meal outdoors, the first night in camp, all arranged and set up and ready to go. He groaned at the idea. And the whole vision repeated itself, the air route less, the arrival nearer, until it was as real as knowledge and tormented him like guilt. He stared at the dead branches slanting over him, the bushes to his left, felt the particled sand under him dirtying his shirt, and listened to a host of flies somewhere buzzing like hornets. They made him all the more aware of his itching bites. It was impossible to just lie there and wait. He crawled out of the lean-to head first and stood up in the sun.

He looked at the southern sky, at the fair-weather cloud at the end of the water and over the green-black horizon. Despite his knowing otherwise, he expected them so vividly it was as if they visited him regularly. He let the feeling stay as long as it lasted. It was illogical, it wasn't time anyway, and they'd never be in that part of the sky. Everything he really knew was negative, only hope was positive, and absurd. He was going to need the absurdity. He sensed, with a twinge of dread, that he had only a loose control over his feelings. It was the lack of food most likely, or withdrawal from the cigarettes, or from the liquor, or just being suddenly cut off from everything. It reminded him he needed a hat, and simultaneously he thought of his handkerchief. He tied a knot in three of its corners, fitted it to his head, tied the fourth knot, and put it on. He giggled, partly in chagrin, as he imagined what he looked like, unshaved, unwashed, disheveled, bites caked with blood, and this white thing on his head sticking out like four hair curlers. It'll do the job though, it'll reflect away a lot of sunlight and a lot of heat. The efficient attitudinizing left him suddenly depressed. Needs weren't funny and makeshift contrivances were bumbling fakes. Equally suddenly he became aghast that all this was actually happening, to him.

"All right, all right"—he spoke as though soothing a disturbed friend—"it's bound to go inside, just leave it alone."

When he was calmer he said weakly: "You better start getting ready."

Unwillingly he set about carrying tinder and twigs to the edge of the water and arranging them so that he could quickly start a big fire. He used only small wood, the smaller the better, took the twigs from the lean-to, from the dwindled pile of firewood, and followed yesterday's wood-dragging path, picking up all the bits and pieces he could find and placing them on the pile. He took off his light shirt, decided against removing his T-shirt, and forced himself to work slowly enough to avoid sweating. He plodded at it, back and forth, until he could find no more twigs. Next he went to the edge of the bush and pulled up small plants by the roots. When he had a substantial armful he dumped them next to the pile of twigs. On a hot fast blaze they'd make a lot of smoke. But one smoke signal wasn't enough, it's ambiguous. He'd need three all lined up and equally spaced to make the fires look intentional.

He wanted to avoid going into the bush for more wood. With only a T-shirt he'd be bitten right through it, and if he dressed fully he'd sweat too much. He had already explored the beach south of the site, and he thought of going north along the lake. Somehow he had to bring himself to make it a special decision as if that direction were taboo. It began to worry him, and he cut the problem short by walking past the site into the new region. It was all strange, a sky he hadn't looked at except at night, a fresh beach, a different bush. He felt he was lost, and he hadn't gone ten yards. He looked back at the site. It was a new angle. But the place was there, the pile of twigs, the sun markers, the lean-to, the familiar bigger rocks. He strolled on, and glanced at his shadow with its grotesque head. Another thing. He took off the hanky, looked at his restored shadow, and put it back on. He wondered what people had done without mirrors and how they had regarded their shadows. Primitive people, what would the sun at high noon have told them? North was the way of shadows, never graced by the sun. He cut that short too and watched the edge of the bush for twigs.

Less than a hundred feet away the beach narrowed to a path, and past this the shoreline turned inland and swung back over hundreds of yards to form a shallow bay. Around it the beach widened and rose in a long sharp slope and ended against a ridge of tough yellowing sod. Behind it was the sky, making the ridge seem higher than it was. As he entered the crescent of the bay he saw dead fallen sections of a huge birch that had probably been struck by lightning. The limbs were dry and brittle, and warm, he noticed when he began snapping off a supply of twigs. The find would save a lot of walking. As he worked he conceived the idea of using a bough with a lot of forks on it as a carrier. He broke one off, propped it upright against the fallen tree, and managed little by little to load it with an intricate tangle of small limbs and twigs. It wasn't too heavy at first, but he had to carry and balance it shoulder-high in order to see where he was going, and that made him tire quickly. In stages he brought it past the first pile, south, about three airplane lengths, dumped it carefully, and prepared tinder under it. The greens he'd get later. He walked slowly back to the fallen birch, still loath to go north, taking the carrier bough with him, and sat down and rested till the sun dried the T-shirt on his back.

He made two more trips with half loads, built a third pile south of the second, and stacked green plants near them. From the site he surveyed his work. He'd be in a hurry to light the first one, it'd have to be big, with a lot of smoke to attract attention. The next two would confirm the signal, no hurry there, unless all three were needed to catch the pilot's eye. That'd all depend: wind direction, reflection, the color of the water, the density of the smoke, competing landmarks. The twigs would burn very quickly and it would take a backup of heavier wood to keep the signal going. He was too tired to gather it, but he started north anyway, just to see.

The walk seemed longer this time. He was retracing steps already taken, reorganizing tasks already done. He felt that everything he did was in a special void, the wood he gathered, the plants he found, the water, the fires he made, the lean-to he had built and unbuilt and rebuilt. No matter how hard he worked, it was all there to be done over again, and more arduously: water a mile away, food even farther, firewood more and more distant, energy lost, and lost again, without being replenished. Diminishing returns, like digging a tunnel in the wrong direction. A vicious circle, spiraling. There'd have to be a way out.

The fallen birch he only looked at. It was too big to be moved. The smaller branches could be snapped off, but the thicker ones would need pounding with a heavy rock. More diminishing returns. It'd be easier to scrounge wood in the bush. Easier, but not easy, and not now. As he moved farther along the bay he realized he was still thinking of the site as central, the place to which everything had to be brought, the place where fires were made. But why not make a fire here? He looked at the fallen tree again. It would be no work at all, no more than making a little tinder and snapping the lighter. A nice reversal. But the blaze would creep along the trunk to the parent tree and from there to the bush. A forest fire was too big a return. The basic idea was good though, and he held on to it. The site wasn't central to anything. He could do things anywhere. And he might even come to need a forest fire. The thought made the place even more ominous.

He got as far as the middle of the bay. It was the wrong time of day to be there. The beach was hot and bleak, a huge gravel pit whose slope rose some twenty feet above him and compounded the glare of the sun. The ridge of yellow sod, dry and dead, ran almost the length of the bay, and the sky behind it was unbroken except for a few treetops that looked too far away to matter. He stood there looking at it, unable to decide what to do. He had to get out of the sun. There was no shade at the site, none on the beach. If he continued north along the shore, he'd probably encounter nothing but more beach and have to come back and start over. It'd be another loss of energy. He decided to gamble on the high ground.

He picked a course with the least obstacles, walked up as far as he could, and began to climb the slope in a long diagonal. He kept slipping on the loose ground, and as he got closer to the top he had to kick out a footing for each step. Finally, at the ridge he leaned over, held on before making the last effort, and dragged himself over the edge. He rested, face-down for a long time, wet, still hot, but knowing it was cooler, and then came to his knees to look around.

It was a clearing, much like the one he had found in the morning, except that the yellow stunted sod was everywhere as if spring had never come. It reminded him of winter kill on the golf course. Out of it grew shrubs and short plants, wildflowers, tall weeds, clumps of high bush like crab-apple trees, and in the distance everything looked green again. To his left, farther north, were five or six isolated pines, too scattered to be a grove, and beyond them more and more trees that finally became a forest. He made his way to the nearest pine and stood in its shadow, relieved, and looked out at the lake. He couldn't see the beach from there. Time asserted itself as sharply as his hunger, as if he hadn't forgotten a minute, and he knew it was around two o'clock. His watch said 2:14.

He could see them at Henri's, almost vividly enough to greet them. The charter plane was landing, or landed, as wish and imagination and knowledge would have it, taxiing to the dock where Henri, or the children, moored it. Eric would get out fast, younger, more eager, followed by Martin, who would almost certainly glance at the children medically and say nothing, and they'd wait for Gerry's great size to ease out of the rocking plane, to look around deliberately and say there's no hurry, we might as well start enjoying it now, Spence has been having all the fun for two days. Hearty vacation greetings, time for a visit, a few drinks, did Spence get away all right? Ah, yes, Mr. Morison got away fine, he's all set for you, he was sure in a good mood, he loves his fishing, you'll have a good time up there, we'll take extra gas for his Cessna if you want to do some exploring.

They're going to do a lot of exploring.

He saw them again and again with variations, different landings from different wind directions, longer taxiings, more or less people at the dock, Gerry getting out first because he was the last and slowest to get in, the charter refueling to go back to Montreal, Henri or his brother getting the other plane ready, the one that would have to search for him, delays over talk and food and the inevitable few drinks, stories of big fish, the high expectation of breaking local records and creating new myths. He could hear them and sense the atmosphere about them, and he felt like a distant ghost who couldn't make contact. He knew everything there was to know—except what was actually happening. They could still be in Montreal. One known fact would make a lot of it real, time all of it.

He was still sweating from his climb, and his breathing hadn't returned to normal. He could hear his heart pounding and his ears ringing, and the physical excitement made his imaginings all the more urgent.

"They—could—have—left—earlier," he said, gasping the words out.

His hair was wet and matted under the knotted hanky. He pulled it from his head and jammed it carefully in his back pocket to make sure no ends could be snagged. He felt less ridiculous with it off, but the action made him suddenly self-conscious, aware somewhat guiltily of a futile vanity, the norm of being seen and being seeable, as though his person were outside him like costume and makeup. He knelt on one knee and tried to rest, uncomfortably, and to watch the horizon with the advantage of some height, but finally he sat down on the compacted pine needles, leaning forward, arms on knees, looking. The new locale made the country strange and impressive, his best view yet of the wilderness. He couldn't dwell on it. The empty southern sky made him impatient, and time was making things happen. The rendezvous that would not take place was too imminent for him to be aware of anything else, and he knew they were flying—or soon to fly—west in that sky about a hundred miles south of him.

The idea was too much. He stood up quickly for fear of missing anything. All he saw was sky.

"They'd be a speck," he whispered, "and they'd have to be at seven thousand feet or more."

He looked at the impossible distance anyway and searched the sky's long edge. It was something he could not avoid doing, and he did it until he satisfied himself that there was nothing to be seen. He was sweating again—getting up suddenly had done that—and he wondered how weak he might have become. He sat down slowly, peeled off the wet T-shirt, and spread it on the tall grasses. He told himself he'd stay put until he was dry and calm and could no longer hear his heart. It gave him a reason for being still.

The slight westerly breeze made him feel cooler, and it seemed to be keeping most of the bugs away. Refracted sunlight moved in the shade around him, and the pines made noises like distant traffic outside a motel window—far-off motors that weren't planes—and it took him a while to identify the source. He looked repeatedly and absently along the grasses in front of him, the slope down to the ridge, the water visible past it, the frustrating skyline, up and back to the long and needled branches over him. The terrain grew less and less hostile, and suddenly it seemed to have lost its strangeness. He could look around and know what to expect. A casual glance took it all in. For a moment he had the feeling that he knew where he was and that he could be at ease there. A calm, peaceful moment. It's a nice spot, his mind intruded, it'd be a good place to make camp, a real camp with tents, not just a survival site, you couldn't make a big fire here, you'd have to . . . He was back to his rush of thinking. He almost got up, but it wasn't time.

Deliberately he looked at the countryside, consciously trying to be at ease again. But it wasn't happening. It kept eluding him like an unrecallable name, the worse for trying. He took to examining the scenery section by section, seeing it pictorially in imaginary frames, pictures for assorted rectangles. A game. It was too artificial. The whole sweep had to be taken in at once, unfocused and unwatched. There was no technique for doing it, except idleness. And it seemed wrong to be idle in an emergency.

He compromised by waiting. He stopped trying to recapture moments or play with the countryside. He waited like a man alert, as if he were watching a radar set. His breathing had become more normal and his face less flushed. As he grew cooler and more rested he felt like relaxing fully and even stretching out on the warm grass. It was a natural urge, the very purpose of a holiday. But he couldn't go that far, he was afraid of being passive, of missing something on the radar set. It didn't matter that all the readings were inside his head.

114

At 3:15 p.m. he decided, against all doubts, that they were arriving at Lac des Grises.

The fiat relieved him. It turned his mind loose and made him take heart. He indulged himself with helping them. The lake was shaped like a flattened boomerang, a rough U-turn in their line of flight. They'd be flying low then, and would have to swing into it before they saw the plane wasn't there. It wouldn't mean anything, I could have gone off on a little sightseeing, but a bell would be ringing, especially with Martin, who was always spotting odd symptoms. Where the hell did he make camp? Do you see anything? It was supposed to be on the east side so we'd have a view of the sunsets. They'd have to decide to scout the lake by flying or by taxiing. Flying, it's faster and easier, if there's something to see. They'd circle once, maybe twice, and see nothing. We better get down there and really take a look. All bells ringing now, landing, only the pilot watching the water, the three others peering at the passing shores. Taxiing, wondering, pull in close, don't cut the engine, there's no point in going ashore till we spot something. Someone would climb on the wing and look around with binoculars, probably Eric, excited, ready to go in all directions. Taxi with him on the wing, he'd want that, and cover the whole perimeter. Nothing. They know something's wrong now, really wrong. The least wrong is a plain mistake, I went to the wrong lake, not likely after the way we poured over maps last winter, but it has to be checked out.

"They'll check the closer lakes."

As he spoke he stopped staring west of south where

Lac des Grises would be. The scenery jumped back into view and the sky was emptier than ever. It was a strange loss, from dream to reality. Yet the dream was substantially true, time was making it so. He kept to his fiat. They were there.

He touched his watch with thumb and forefinger and calculated the time for a search of two possible lakes. He made a schedule totaling a half hour, certain that the events were taking place. Time felt like a reality in itself, a basic resource. It made things go, made everything go in fact, and on time, wrong if not on time, and you had to respond to it, move with it, use it. Mere waiting did not fit this, it was too negative, as if non-time were unreality and waiting a sort of nothingness. And yet, earlier, a moment without time had come to him. Yeah, and I thought I was at home in this place.

With a sort of active calmness, like an actor in control, he waited out the events on the schedule. It was a way of keeping everything else at arm's length. It minimized the tension between his vivid daydreaming and his actual perception, the shifts from what he wished to what he really knew. He felt better now. He was cool and dry, as was his T-shirt, which he put on, and his breathing was normal. He was rested and relatively fit.

But hunger chewed at him again. This time it was sharper, as demanding as a shout, and painful enough to make him fearful of being weak. And with it came an urgency in his bowels that he couldn't ignore. He got up quickly, disoriented, and cast about for a likely place. He didn't want to do it in the open. Why not? Was a man vulnerable at stool? There was little time for argument. He managed to get some ten paces from the tree and slip his clothes down and squat. He was afraid of diarrhea, to be sick here would be disastrous. Urine was a problem in that position. Quickly he put his hand under him and directed the stream away from his clothes. The rest wasn't diarrhea. He stayed in the silly squat and looked for something that would do for paper; a broadleaf plant a dozen yards away. Holding his pants at his knees, he waddled over to it and took enough leaves to do the job cleanly. Did the modern bathroom, he asked himself, evolve from the primitive fear of being attacked? He dressed with relief. Another thing to plan for, a paper substitute.

He went back to the pine and checked his schedule. It was 4:06.

They've searched the lakes by now. And found nothing. They'd radio the news ahead and fly back to Chibougamau, low and slow, looking below for a signal or a downed plane. They know.

"They know I'm not there, they know I'm missing."

It sounded childish. He really didn't know they knew. And to himself he wasn't missing, he was here.

11

He had to give in to his hunger. It preoccupied him. It disrupted his thoughts and made any position uncomfortable. It seemed to come in long pulses, threatening like appendicitis, and the awkward rhythm made him anticipate the spasms. With each wave he felt a sudden vicious anger, an urge to act quickly and violently. It was so strong it surprised him almost to laughter. As he adverted to it and understood it, the anger subsided but not the hunger. What a bawling out a waiter would get, that's why they serve drinks, it cuts the appetite and keeps the peace. He moved without thinking into the fields behind the pines, noting the direction east. He kept his eyes to the ground, walking slowly, looking for the tiny yellow flowers that hadn't harmed him so far. Lunch over twenty-four hours ago and crises and hard work and a mouthful of greens this morning, the stuff in the shirt is probably wilted and no good, another mistake.

He wasn't as cautious this time, or as ignorant. He spotted the flowers quickly, elated by his minimum know-how, pulled up a plant, broke off parts, and began chewing without hesitation. He chewed thoroughly. It'll take time, it's slower than wolfing food from a plate, and it's probably wiser this way. The hunger stayed, even increased. An entree, a salad, without oils and the rest of it, the buns, and butter, tomato juice, the shrimp cocktail, a whole meal right there. He meandered as he ate, it seemed to help, halting for a while and moving on, a sort of peristalsis. He discovered that the younger plants were tastier and more tender, and he looked for them in earnest as he chewed, not picking a fresh one until it was time to eat it. Searching and chewing and waiting became a pattern, regular and repetitious, a monotony, and not unenjoyable, it yielded results. He paused longer as he looked, knelt on one knee instead of stooping to pick the plants, lingered over his choices. More moments without time, unnoticed. His hunger abated and became appetite, and stayed. It would never be satisfied this way. The greens should be cooked, he'd be able to eat more of them if they were. A plain kitchen pot seemed like an unattainable work of genius.

He foraged until he began to wonder what quantity his stomach could tolerate. It was a drastic change in diet, from prepared and processed food to raw wild vegetation, fine for nature cranks and animals, but it felt wrong. Everything else was wrong anyway, so maybe this didn't matter. The pines seemed far away, clustered and not so big. He guessed he had covered about a quarter of a mile, and as he started back he re-membered time. It was after five. They were at Chi-bougamau by now, getting ready to organize a search. The thought troubled him somehow. Scheduling would be difficult, they had a range of choices in meth-ods and timing, and he couldn't guess which ones they'd pick except that they'd be searching and search-ing over a line of flight he had never taken. It would take long, and they would persist, and be wrong. It was going to be a different sort of waiting.

Near the pines he remembered his need for paper and turned to his right in search of more broadleaves. Past the scene of his last emergency he saw them grow-ing in scattered abundance, sticking up over the tall grasses, big rhubarblike leaves, some about the size of an opened *Time* magazine. He tugged at them, hoping to collect them fast, but the leafy sections tore and slid along the stalk, leaving him with a handful of wet green mash. The job couldn't be hurried. He broke the stalks one by one near the ground or near the main stem and tossed them into a pile. The air thickened with disturbed bugs. Still he didn't hurry. To be hot and sweating would make them ravenous. He kept at the task with a sort of greed, every stalk was one more in hand, one less to get later, and these he could store, even hoard, and they might be better dried out. What are you going to do, carry them around with you? Dry them and roll them up? Or maybe trim them nice and square like the real thing, uh? He was stopped by a helpless unvoiced guffaw. And weak with absurdity he gathered them one by one into his left arm like an enormous bouquet and walked back partly toward the pines on his way to the ridge. There he sat down to slip over the edge, got his footing on the gravel and scrambled down the slope. The beach was still hot and glaring, the sun not as high. He was serious again. He was intent on getting back to the site, on time.

He was near the fallen birch when he realized that he was pressing on. He slacked his pace and adjusted the load of leaves. There was no hurry, he'd already had supper. There's nothing to be on time for, you're not going to *eat* this stuff. But reasoning made no difference, he couldn't saunter: it's got to be before six. Evening begins after that.

When he got to the site he tried to look at his watch but his left arm was buried in the leaves. They'd tangle if he dropped them in a pile and they wouldn't dry, they'd rot. So one by one and by the stalks he spread them on the rocks and gravel over an area the size of a couple of beds. They added to the general debris. It was ten to six. The sun was across the lake, ready to get low. The shadows of the markers pointed roughly to the lean-to, and the three piles of signal wood stood out in the crosslighting. The cigarettes were still damp and brown like something in a public urinal, and the stripped pack looked like somebody's litter. There was nothing to sit on except rocks and twigs, and despite his arrival on time and his fatigue he had no end-of-the-day feeling. Evening was simply not beginning. Evening meant being out of contact with work, past the rush-hour traffic, at home with a drink before supper or looking forward to dining out. Habit and routine made evening. It wouldn't happen here, six o'clock meant nothing, the end of day would come with night.

He couldn't wait out the non-evening. He toured the site as though checking it, but there was nothing to check, no tent supports, no moorings, no gear to be stowed. The crude assemblages of broken wood and stones made the place look desolate. It bore the traces of the last twenty-four hours and reminded him of how absent he was from everything he knew. It said nothing of the future. He walked south along the lakeside, stopping to look for flotsam and saw none, it'd be a miracle to have that stuff float to shore, and he wasn't swimmer enough to go after it, or well-fed enough, that'd be another miracle. He gave only a glance at the skies, watching belonged to the high ground under the pines, and wishing had given way to waiting. There were facts yet to be faced, the pressure of truth unreleased. It was too early to stop wishing.

"I hope they don't tell you too soon."

It was out before he knew it. He saw his wife agonized with worry as they searched, and the words came with the image. No, no, they'll handle it right.

"It's just below the surface, isn't it?"

Maybe I should let it come up. No, it's pure emotion, you don't want to get thrown, you've got enough as it is.

Yeah.

He stared at the water awhile and stepped away from his thoughts. He went, not quickly for he'd learned that lesson, to the space that led into the bush, paused to see if the bugs were active, and started to look for likely evergreens, flat, soft, unspiky, not the Christmas-tree kind. He found what he thought was a young tree, a tall straight thing about ten feet high with branches starting full and wide near the ground and coning toward the top. Its sprays were flat and had smooth scalelike leaves. And it was tough. The branches wouldn't break and the sprigs didn't snap off, they had to be twisted and tortured. It was going to be a long job, with the penknife. He fell on the system of bending a sprig away from the bough and slicing through it in two strokes. It was one by one again, no speed, just progress. He let them accumulate on the ground. The bugs found him quickly. He didn't hurry. When he had enough for a double armful he gathered them and walked back to the site and dumped them near the lean-to. He put on his light shirt, returned to the entrance to the bush, put on the knotted hanky, and went back to work. He kept cutting until he had a heap of sprigs. This he moved to the beach in two loads, rested a little, and got them to the site in two trips. He took off hanky and shirt and leaned on the big rock to contemplate the project. The work had taken a long time and, in his condition, a lot of effort. The rest of it ought to be fairly easy.

He removed his belongings from the lean-to, cleared the remaining twigs, which he saved for tinder, and spread the evergreen sprigs to a likely thickness and stretched out to test the bedding. It was comfortable, but it would mat. He crawled out, added more sprigs, didn't test it again, and put the rest of them outside at the base of the lean-to as something to sit on. It made a good pile which compressed when he sat on it to the height of a low footstool. It seemed like a lot of trouble, but it was better than getting sore on the gravel. The sun was low, slightly to his right, a little north of west, perhaps a half hour away from the horizon. It was 7:48. He didn't reminisce about yesterday's crises, he knew them, and that was enough. He was better off now, in a way.

There were still things to do. He got up tiredly and set about preparing wood for the night's fire. He felt the stress of having to do everything newly. He laid out tinder, twigs, the smaller boughs, and lined up the bigger pieces so they could be fed in easily. The supply had thinned out. He wouldn't need a big fire, and he could use pieces from the lean-to, it wasn't much of a shelter anyway. He went to the cigarettes, carefully corded them in the container section of the package, now dry, which he kept opened and flat, and carried that and the sleeve to a spot where they would get heat from the fire. He thought of trying one now, but he wanted to save lighter strokes. Near the lean-to where he had placed his belongings he dumped the greens from his heavy shirt and draped it on the lean-to. With everything organized he sat down on the evergreen cushion and loosened his boots. On second thought he removed them completely and took off his socks to keep them from collecting sand. A small thing, but it felt good, more like the end of day than mere time. He had done a lot of walking.

They're probably using two planes. One slow one

for a good look and one faster for a bird's-eye view before nightfall. They'd know it was the second night. If I was down there I'd hear them and see them and send up signals. But they see none. At least four passes, the one just going, which would be heard below, the one coming back to base, which'd be a search, then the real search and back, and maybe another, it depends on when they started. No signals. So they're looking for wreckage. It's hard to see from a thousand feet. A landing strip, a clearing, a lake tells you where to look and you find things. But the bush hides everything. So they'll keep doing it again and again. And never be sure. Days. On one of those days they'd have to figure: he has all that gear—if he's not able to signal, he is not able to survive. They wouldn't give up, they'd look for the body.

It was a strange bit of realism. Hypothetical, and from their point of view. It didn't touch him subjectively until he turned it around: if the body's here, they'll never find it. The crows would get it, and the weather. He was a little awed by the magnitude of the "if."

"A lot would depend on the menu."

The heavy flippancy was a way of not going into it. He knew where he stood. He couldn't plan for food, he could only look, for greens at that, and those he had to eat raw. He couldn't even boil water, he didn't have a pot to put it in. The clichés evoked a twinge of grim humor, jokes that required civilization. He'd need something he could roast over a fire, an animal, or a fish. And that would have to be by accident, for there was no way of doing it consistently. Planning was a form of worrying. He gave up on it.

It was well after eight. The sun was a few diameters away from setting, and the sky was clear except for a scattering of fair-weather clouds. He wondered if they would fly at night. All that trouble for a fire that wasn't there. He put on his socks and boots, tying them loosely, and went to get his sport shirt. He was putting it on when the idea came to him, a sudden flash of an idea for containing water, not boiling it, not yet, but at least holding it in one place. He examined the concept and said, "Yes!"—a hole in the ground lined with leaves, broadleaves, which weren't really toilet paper.

He slipped the shirt off and put it back on the rock. The hole he could picture and how he'd try to arrange the leaves, but the rest was a problem: where to put it and how to get water to it. And then a bigger question that threatened to veto the whole thing: why bother at all? What was the point of having a hole full of water? Not drinking water, it'd get stagnant. Confusion and doubt replaced what had been a good clear notion. He felt balked, and resented it. But the idea was still promising, and he decided to try it out. He'd dig near the fire, so the hole could be seen when it got dark.

About three feet from the prepared firewood he knelt on the gravel and began scooping some of it aside with his bare hands. He didn't get far, and it was work he could ill afford to do. He stopped and found a heavy stick, which he sharpened to a point. By pressing with this he was able to loosen the dirt, and when enough

126

was dug he scooped it to build up the sides a little above ground level. He made a hole about eight inches deep, two feet wide at the top, and sloping down to a bottom the size of a dinner plate. He firmed up the sides with stones, and as he was doing that the rest of the idea came to him, and he knew he had been right in persisting: he could heat water with hot stones.

He selected about ten leaves, noticing that the sun had gone down, and carefully trimmed the stalks off with his penknife. The roundest and flattest he placed on the bottom of the hole. Overlapping it and sloping down the side he put another, then another overlapping both, and so on, shingle style, until the sides were completely covered. It took a lot of leaves. They didn't fit well, the slightest gap meant using a whole leaf, and he couldn't force them into place. The resulting bowl looked fragile. Water could shift the leaves and seep into the ground, a stone ill-placed could tear them. It needed another layer. Patiently he trimmed more shingles, almost exhausting the supply, laid out a second center piece, and repeated the whole operation. Gently he pressed the layers together to remove what air he could, and decided to leave it alone. There goes my paper, I'll have to go in the lake and wipe my ass with water. My hands too. It was ready for testing.

The only thing that could carry water was his boots. He scuffed out a clear path to the water's edge, sat down to remove them, and in the instant decided to use only one, better keep the other dry. He put the sock and felt sole in his side pockets, found he'd have to wade, stopped, removed the other boot, and rolled up his pants legs. It was turning out to be a complicated affair. In bare feet he waded to calf depth, filled the boot, and pranced back as fast as he could, trying not to spill too much water. At the hole he broke the force of the water by pouring it into his left hand and letting it trickle onto the leaves. He stopped and pressed the leaves, poured, stopped and pressed again. Soon he was pouring on the back of his hand while he kept the leaves from moving, and he emptied the boot in one flow. He watched the level. It seemed to be holding. But a bootful wasn't much water. He went to get another, and emptied that. It held. He needed a third. And that too held. It brought the level about two-thirds of the way up. He estimated he might have three quarts of water. He hobbled to the lake for his dry boot, put them both on, wet or not, and stayed sitting awhile to look at the holeful of water. It was like discovering fire.

From the lake he got four stones the size of grape-fruits, why the lake he didn't know except that it seemed cleaner that way, made sure they were free of grit, and shoved them under the firewood and facing the water hole. He retrieved his sport shirt, put it on as he had been doing before all the work began, and with tinder and lighter, careful to use one stroke, he lit the fire and gratefully stumbled back to his seat. Measured in time and salary, his salary, it was a very costly routine. But the materials were free. And it was better than last night when he had started naked. The fire made the twilight darken. He could hear a variety of birds, their sounds quite separable, and he became aware of the busy insects and his constant itching. To the side, away from the fire, he saw rises breaking the glossy lake, the fish were feeding. He got up, with effort, and strolled to the water's edge to see better. The rises said it all, on vacation they were the peak of anticipated enjoyment. Big ones, probably trout. Here, the fish remained themselves, a part of nature he couldn't touch without special tools. He stood a long while watching, noticed the thin crescent moon about to set, and went back to feed the fire and sit down.

His fatigue held him there this time. He didn't want to do anything more. But the rock-and-water trial had to be completed. He thought of putting it off till tomorrow, but that would waste fuel and gas and time and the water'd probably need changing and he'd want dry boots then. Another lesson: twilight's no time to start things. Fine. How many twilights do you think you're . . . ? The speculation was back.

Timing would be important. Just when to make smoke during the day, when to make the three fires at night. And that was when they'd be near enough to spot it. And *when* would *that* be? Not tonight, that's sure. By now they've probably notified Search and Rescue, and in the morning the Air Force would take over. They'd do a fifty-mile swath centered on the Lac des Grises line. Not enough. And they'd have to have good reason to deviate from it.

On all fours he cleared a space in front of him and smoothed it out. Using a stick, he marked Chibougamau near his left knee, and three feet straight out from this toward the fire he set down Lac des Grises. Close to him on his right, forming a right-angle triangle he made a point and drew in the three sides. Somewhere along the hypotenuse, close to himself, he planted the stick to mark his own likely position. He stared at the crude map, finally sat back, and tried to be precise about the course he had taken. It had been a fun thing. Spur of the moment. Around Mistassini, northeast. Then the swing-around to roughly southwest. And then? In distance, in time, how far? He couldn't be sure. The fire needed stoking, it had a base of big hot coals. The stones would be ready.

He didn't rush into it, he'd worked too hard to have it fail now. The problem was getting the stones into the delicate basin without mishap. The mounded side of the hole was an obstacle, a hard push would break it or cause the stones to tear the leaves. He should have built it flat. But he had built it deep enough: he noticed that the water was below ground level and that the mound was not really needed. Carefully he lifted the leaves, dug out a channel that sloped into the hole, and fitted the leaves back into it. He continued the channel as far as he could toward the fire. And that seemed to solve that. The next thing was a stick that could give him some measure of control. He finally decided on a limb that forked into three branches. These he broke off near the fork to make a stumpy misshapen trident. He poked a stone out of the coals, nudged it slowly down the channel, stopped, quickly got a second stick, and using both he eased the stone into the water. It sizzled and steamed and finally looked hot and wet where it showed above the water level. He tested the water, it was hot, like shaving water, but it hadn't boiled.

He sat where he was. He felt low and discouraged. Would three more rocks do it? He didn't dare use them all up. He had to narrow down the factors. Maybe there was too much water, or the rock wasn't heated enough, or it cooled on the way over. He decided there was too much water. He flapped a lot of it out, felt the stone, and quickly took it out. He went near the lean-to where he had dumped the greens from his bush shirt, got most of them, shook them free of sand, and put a quantity of them in the water. He lined up the three rocks in the fire and rolled them one by one, with violent hissing, into the water. It boiled. And kept boiling for a while. He was too fascinated to think of timing it. When rocks and water and greens were simply making vapor, he sharpened a small stick and fished out a sample of the greens. He blew on it, put it in his palm, and ate it from there. It was tender, not stringy, and tasted the way he imagined boiled lettuce would taste. One stick wasn't enough. He made another. With one in each hand he could lift the greens but he had nothing to put them on. He placed a broadleaf on the ground and ate from it with his fingers. The stuff was food, it was hot, and it was compressed into usable quantities. He ate all of it with a sense of climax, but not fullness. It was almost fully dark, 10:17, a red glow still in the west. It seemed he had worked all day to reach this point, and then by a series of accidents. All day for a part of a meal. He'd have to organize it better.

He put wood on the fire, closed in the longer pieces, and went back to his seat, where, feeling cooler, he put on his bush shirt. The working day was finally at an end. The first full day after touchdown. Some touchdown. T plus one. He remembered the cigarettes. Up again. He felt like crawling. He got them, pulled a light from the fire, and puffed and smoked. It didn't keep its promise, it made him dizzy and weak. Reluctantly he threw it into the fire and put the pack in his shirt pocket. One gone, twenty left. It sounded like a bad omen.

He stared at the crude map in the sand, four small depressions that passed for points, one for him, and shaky little rivulets that meant lines. He scratched in an estimated fifty-mile swath. It passed only twenty-five miles north of Chibougamau, and he'd been a hundred miles north of it. They'd never look that far. They have no way of guessing, unless somebody saw me, and heard the news, and remembered, and said something. They can't reconstruct my actions, they weren't logical, I was taking a break, on holiday. I went sightseeing. Why did I ever—? I felt like it, I was feeling good after a few drinks. Would they guess that? A few, perfectly normal, a beer at the hotel, a round with Gus and his friends, no, it was two draft at the hotel, and two more, a round of four with Gus, and another round, then Scotch at Henri's, then . . . In the plane. He tried to dismiss it, but it came back. That's a lot of drinking. Yes, but it's not a big thing, I've done it often, it's just about average for a guy who drinks. It might be, but it's still a lot of drinking. You were drunk. Ah, get off it, I've seen guys take . . .

But the fact had come home.

"Drunk!" he shouted to the faint horizon. It was like

a furious curse at things. He was on his feet. "You hear me? Drunk!"

Big professional. Wise guy. He was close to tears.

He waited to regain some of his composure. Then he put the hanky on his head to keep the bugs at bay and crept into the lean-to for what he hoped would be a long sleep.

12

The evergreen couch was adequate, a lot better than twigs. It settled under his weight and prodded him in places, but he was too tired to track down the offending sprigs, they'd eventually bend anyway. It kept him well off the ground and gave the impression of warmth. He wondered what kind of evergreen it was, not pine, not balsam, not fir, they're supposed to be big, there's spruce and cedar and hemlock, only words for him, he knew the shape of his tree, the sprays and flattened leaves, and he'd recognize it. That and the plant with the little yellow flowers. For all his outdoorsman sports he didn't know much about these things, there was always someone around to say that's a such-and-such tree and the Indians made a medicinal tea from that plant, and it really didn't matter, it was interesting, and sounded like a tour, nature had become a museum. And a playground. That's what brought me out here. I'll have to find out what those things are. I wonder who told the Indians. And how did they ever manage to boil tea?

Past the last branch over his head he could see the stars in a piece of sky. The lean-to was an obstacle. It didn't amount to much, it wouldn't keep off the night air and it blocked the heat from the fire. Useless against bugs and animals and rain. And yet it felt right to be inside it, it was a hole to crawl into. If that was all, he'd have to learn to do without it, to leave the nest, the cave, the surrogate womb, abandon the illusion of a psychological shelter, in trouble it would be a disadvantage, a shelter can also be a trap, cozy, bundled, tied in, it assumed a protector, a mama, a group, a community, what he was to his family. No, he wasn't a protector, he was a supplier of funds, a provider of technological devices, a way to tap the service environment, what had happened to the human, to the engulfing love that . . . ? Without the lean-to he'd be able to see the entire sky. Tomorrow. There's lots to do. It has to be planned in the right sequence and done at the right time or you'll work and work and work at walking and searching and lugging dead trees and collecting paper and digging and stripping branches and rolling rocks. He created fire and water and invented chopsticks and he was looking for something past the last limb where the heavens were. The lean-to was moved away and he saw the entire range of sky above him, the stars all giving signals in a universe that was very alert.

He couldn't understand why the stars were signals. They were bright with emergency and they made him afraid, a skyful of unanticipated dangers. And suddenly he realized it was because he was flying. He was in his own plane, heading south and west—the direction seemed important—and he was looking and looking, he then knew, for the other plane with Martin and the others and he had no intention of landing because somehow that wasn't part of it. Just the flying, and the looking, and the simultaneous sense of wandering deep within himself, an involuted universe where he was trying to build fires, signals sent and seen, and the felt presence of his children, the years and years of love slipping away. Contradiction tugged at him like turbulence. You've got nothing to fly with, you're gonna have to postpone your holidays. A long reef of rocks made the water boil as he approached it, but he missed it this time and flew free and chuckled at the boiling water and he felt there was something wrong until he realized the plane was gone. Quickly he checked the stars. They were still there. In a while he was flying again, but he knew the cycle was going to return, air, rocks, water, nothing, and it did, ever narrowing, loss and gain merging into something unknown.

He was surprised to see his wife there. They were underwater with aqualungs and flashlights and they were pulling things from a sunken plane that looked like a moving van. It was some kind of sport, they were on vacation in the Bahamas, no surprise any more, and he was enjoying breathing through the mouthpiece. They unpacked light switches and he turned them on to light up the picnic table, the frozen food had thawed, the tents were dry. She said, why are you bringing so much stuff? We're going in style with all the comforts. They hauled out a shipping carton with printing on the sides that said it was full of bathroom tissue. The conversation bothered him, you're not supposed to talk with these things on. They extricated a casting rod and an automatic clothes washer. She laughed at the washer, for me? You have a whole lakeful of water, do your washing in that. The aqualung became heavy on his back and he had to leave in a hurry and hold his breath in the pressing darkness. Betty, don't worry. But he was gone from her. He tried and tried to go back but his efforts put him on a shore where the sky held down horizons of sheer terror. He started digging a big hole for reasons he hadn't quite figured out, and then nothing.

The whole atmosphere said that he was in his office, he was sure of it, and yet he knew he wasn't there. He was struggling in a regularized fury to get the phone to work. He wasn't angry, it wasn't a matter for anger, it was a question of skill, and power. He had it laid out on his desk, all the parts organized and understood, for they'd held courses about it, but it wouldn't work. From somewhere low voices muttered, conference voices heavy with policy, the motion reads, all in favor. Men in city work clothes, with a moving van downstairs, came in casually to clear out his office and ignored him completely. He wasn't there. They took out a lot of furniture, the accumulation on the way up, none of it really his, and finally the desk with the phone pieces on it. You can't do that, I didn't authorize a move. They left only the big windows with Montreal outside them. His secretary didn't answer him, didn't even hear him, nor her assistant, nor the directors still mumbling in the other room, nor the other executives, his friends, who had their social-business faces on, creations of the company, all in favor. All right, I won't pee with you guys any more. He tracked things down to a long quiet lake where beyond the quiet was an infinite energy. He was wholly there now, but he'd forgotten why, and he made plans to dive for the moving van. Down. Way down. Perhaps not to return.

The twitching in his legs stirred him a little. He knew he was sleeping and he wanted to sleep much longer. But a spasm jerked his whole body and woke him suddenly and clearly. He thought he was fully awake until he tried to move. He was too heavy, and he was glad of it. It was very dark. He couldn't see anything. Automatically he reached up and touched the branches overhead. The whole lean-to shook. He turned a little to his right and was able to peer through the crevices at the dim glow of the burning-out fire. With a mental groan and a real sigh he felt the burden of having to get up and stoke it. Not yet, let it wait. The night sounds made him know where he really was, and it pained him to realize it. Somewhere on a hypotenuse. He remembered he had been dreaming, no more, and he looked at the stars with feelings that hadn't worn off.

Let it go out, it isn't that cold. He closed his eyes and tried to sleep again, but his mind was too busy.

"It's bad enough during the day."

Languidly he turned on his right side, sliding himself back to stay in the same spot, slumped awhile, and

138

twisted himself face-down and crawled out of the lean-to. He made a lot of subjective noise, and he wasn't trying to be silent. Something, an animal certainly, darted away along the gravel and into the bush. A trap would do it. Just set it and wait. Complete with extra-length noncorrosive chain, at your local outfitter's. Easy. He was on his feet. Don't let the nature freaks see you buying it. The night wasn't as dense outside, and he knew what to expect, how to walk on the visible but unseen ground, how to reach for things that had no distance. He stepped past the red-hot ashes, he wanted to keep his night vision, and walked flat-footed to the lake. It shone like a tin roof and seemed to be tilted toward him. The Milky Way looped the whole sky with its stars. It went southwest. Unbelievable to have so many. Unbelievable to die.

It was just a thought, a bit of philosophizing, not an expression of his fears. He sensed his way along the shore and turned inland a little where he stopped to urinate. How's that for coming down to earth? A pee will do it every time, you can tell how a conference is going by how the delegates behave at the urinals, pausing to chat or hurrying to wash up and get out or pretending great effort as if they all had a dose of clap. He wondered what the animals made of his traces. Another creature territorializing, and taking up a lot of their ground. A creature with fire and a funny nest. There'd be wolves up here, and maybe bears. Just let's everybody mind his own business. He couldn't pass up the fire, it had to give signals, however small. He put twigs on the hot ashes, waited till they flamed, added what branches he could find. He felt heavy all over. He ducked into the shelter on all fours and turned on his back in one smooth motion. He was getting good at it. He let gravity do the rest. I wonder how deep that plane is. Down. Way down. He fully expected to dream.

13

The morning told him he was still there. He looked at blue sky where the stars had been, and he knew there was sunlight on the lake. The birds were busy in the woods. Spiders had made webs on the bushes next to him. There was no wind. He was stiff and sore, and his thoughts were far away. The lean-to exasperated him. He turned painfully, without exercising his muscles, and got out. He was dirty and itchy and wished he could shave. The something he felt on his head was the knotted hanky. He shoved it in his pocket. It was taking a long time to get awake.

He recognized the evening's work, the leaves and rocks in the hole, the water gone, another problem, the few unused broadleaves, the channel, the ashes and a wisp of smoke, the map. It was like having a hangover. The map made him look skyward at nothing. Nothing except miles of clear sky.

"They've got perfect visibility."

He said it casually, as if it didn't matter. It was too
early to get worked up about it. The far shore was
brightly lit, and almost all of the lake. Nothing floated
on it. A vague idea about diving came and went. The
beach and the site were in shade, a little cool, and there
seemed to have been no dew. It was ten past seven.
The second day after touchdown, the third without
contact. He wound his watch as a way of getting things
started. It only made him aware of how tired he was.

The day needed planning. And he gave thought to it.
It had to go by on two assumptions: that they would fly
in this area, and that they wouldn't. If they did he had
only to watch and signal, if they didn't he had to get
more food. And if he was out getting food he couldn't
light the signal fires. It doesn't take long for a plane to
fly by. And it could happen. They could let Search and
Rescue do the fifty-mile thing and they could rent a
helicopter and go wandering all over. Several helicop-
ters, we've got the resources. And Henri could put up
two or three amphibians. And they could radio anybody who might be out camping, and alert those who
were just starting out. A big fan, spider-web style, a
quarter of it would do, a right angle, with a hypotenuse. But the speculation gave him nothing, except
hope. The first plan was to wash.

He went to the shore and stripped and shivered his
way into the water. He washed and shivered again as
he came out. It was no boys'-camp stuff, it was getting
complicated. He tried to squeegee the water from his
body, but that only spread it out, the day wasn't hot
enough to evaporate it. He'd have to wash at high

noon, if another noon had to go by. Finally he fished out the T-shirt and drawers, used these as a towel, washed them and laid them out on the small boulders. He put on the rest of his clothes before he was fully dry. He was weak and shaky after the cleanup, it had been vigorous exercise, and he was hungrier than ever. The hunger was always there, it varied only in intensity. He had to ignore it for now and keep planning out his moves. He drank lake water to save walking a mile to the stream.

He traced the wisp of smoke to a smoldering hunk of branch, cleared the ashes from it, and blew it into a glow. He moved it out of the ash pile, kept it going, and fed it tinder and twigs. He worked slowly, in a deliberate dawdle, like a boy with nothing to do. He pushed the ashes to one side, and in their place he put the stones from the water hole and about a dozen more from around the beach. On this he built up wood for a fire. He put the remaining broadleaves over the old ones in the hole and cleared the channel to the stones. He checked the stick to push with and the sticks to serve with. The water could wait. It was easy enough to boot it from the lake. He'd need broadleaves and greens. Later he'd need firewood. He sat down, and rested, and planned the timing. The fire could last for about an hour. There was no hurry, except for his hunger. He lingered and watched and stared southwest. Finally from the mini-fire he lit the wood over the stones and began walking north to the pines. He made a note of the time: 8:05.

The fallen birch and the bay looked different, they

had deep shadows in the morning light and the ridge seemed higher than yesterday's estimate of twenty feet. He decided against climbing it and went to the far end of the bay where the slope ended at water level. When he turned to walk back along the ridge he heard the faint trickle of running water. He detoured, still north along the shore, and found a shallow gravelly stream about six feet wide emptying into the lake. He didn't stop over it, he was on a schedule. The walk had eaten up over ten minutes.

He cut the broadleaves at their stalks to save a second operation and stacked them on his bush shirt under the pine tree. In the field he stripped to the waist, made a small clearing for his sport shirt, and used that as a place for dumping the greens. He was organized to do the job quickly, but there were bees around the wildflowers, which were everywhere, and he had to move slowly to avoid them. At times he was forced to stop completely, and he was soon behind schedule. What he was losing was watching time, the fire he could always remake. He looked at the sky and considered and decided in favor of food. He began eating some of the greens as he collected them, and he kept on the move like a browsing animal. He figured the bees would be used to that. He wondered where they were hiving. He merely toyed with the idea, it would be hard work tracking their flight, and dangerous to try to steal their honey. But honey was almost all sugar, and sugar was energy. He'd need smoke, which he could make, and netting and gloves, impossible, it was a special craft with special tools.

"The nectar."

With something of a sly grin he plucked an orange flower, checked it for insects and any sort of nettle, and ate it. It was like thin sweet fluffy paper, about as substantial as a mouthful of fog. The stuff might convert to sugar. He tried another, and another, and a pale blue one. The grin stayed, it was like putting something over on the bees. He could see himself sitting on his front lawn eating his wife's peonies. Spence! what are you doing? I'm eating flowers. And he laughed. And she laughed. And remained in his mind. He felt like speaking to her.

It was after ten when he got back to the site. The shade had shrunk to a thin strip along the woods and everything had gotten warm. He tended to the fire, the leaves, the cooking water, and watched the skies as he worked. In another half hour he was eating: the greens boiled and the flowers raw for fear of losing their nectar in the water. It was very late for breakfast. He'd have to store a supply of greens, lost vitamins or not, just to have something to eat when he got up. It assumed the worst, but so did hunger. When the water cooled he drank a lot of it with his hands. Thin soup. It saves a lot of walking and it's full of something or other. He sat on the sprig cushion and watched. His wife was very present in his mind, and he felt sure they had told her the news.

The sun got higher and hotter. His eyes hurt with the glare. And he knew he couldn't stay at the site. He had forgotten about the noon heat on the open beach, and he hadn't made plans for it. He did now. He dismantled the lean-to, something he should have done when it was cool, and spread the small logs near the water in two parallel rows about ten feet apart. They covered about forty feet. The last two, on the north end, he joined in an arrowhead. Three piles of wood and the pointer. He'd be over there. From the air it'd look like three dots and a matchstick. He put rotten wood and vegetation on the fire to make it smoke. It gave a third dimension to the signal. He took his laundry from the boulders, his two shirts, put on the hanky, and walked once more to the bay. There he washed his socks, left them on the beach to dry and continued, booted, to the end of the ridge and up to the pines. At his old place he put his underwear back on, and as he belted his pants he noticed that his waist had gone in by two notches. That was at least two inches on his belt. In a vague way he was glad, the sort of thing you'd brag about at the Y, but it worried him. He took off the headgear, put his boots back on in case he had to make a run for it, and sat down to resume his vigil.

He could see the smoke he'd made. It rose over the woods to his left and seemed closer than it was. He looked with purpose to the right of it, along the horizon, and up and back. There was nothing. He did it again and again, and tried to make it routine, but it was difficult to maintain. He learned to screen out birds and bugs and the tricks of his own eyes, and he held his desires in check as the successive moments felt more and more crucial. It was a phony crisis, time had nothing to do with it, he wasn't waiting for a plane that was late. He was watching for one that might not be there at all. Eventually he relaxed the intensity of his searching and simply looked at the southwest. And as time went by, he leaned against the pine and stretched out his legs. He vetoed the idea of sleeping, he couldn't take that much of a chance. He rested as he was and kept staring in the distance. It made no difference. Nothing happened.

Around three he was too hungry to sit still. Keeping the sky in sight, he explored the area between the ridge and the pines. He nibbled at the usual greens and collected them, going back and forth to his shirts under the tree. It was hot work no matter how slowly he went. He had to cover his head and not stay too long in the sun. There were very few bees, but birds the size of sparrows fluttered over him in protest, some with red markings, and they seemed to have nests in the tall weeds. He kept seeing small red berries here and there close to the ground and finally picked one. It was small, hardly as large as a small peanut, and it tasted sour and vaguely familiar—wild strawberries, he should have known. They were too small and scarce to collect. He ate them as he went along, and then took to plucking the plants and eating the berries in the shade as he watched. He felt a little guilty at the waste, as though he should be superstitious about it, but it got him off his knees and out of the sun and it saved a lot of time. Even at that, he felt his criteria were irrelevant. But he kept doing it and he kept watching. The still unseen plane was more real than the countryside.

Later, past four when he glanced at his watch, he cut some broadleaves and carried everything down along

the ridge to the beach at the northern end of the bay.
On impulse he put his baggage in the shade and started for the stream he had seen in the morning. Then he
stopped and looked along the lake to the southwest.
He'd be under cover if he went in, he wouldn't see,
and it would be hard to hear over the sound of the water, however gentle. But he wasn't on a schedule this
time, he was free. And it wasn't just for fun, he was dependent on what he could find, by accident. Despite
the good reasons, he couldn't decide to be out of sight
of the sky. He had watched too long, and it would be a
fatal irony if they came now and missed him. *If* they
came. And if they didn't, and he had left areas unex-
plored while the weather was good and he had a little
food in his stomach . . . He put a stop to the debate
and gave himself a choice of yes or no. He chose yes,
but first he checked the horizon like a man looking for
snipers, and gave himself a time limit for exploring, at
most ten minutes, then out, then maybe five more.

He took his boots off, rolled up his pants legs, and all
but tiptoed into the water. The stream was cold and the
bush was cool, both welcome. He crept cautiously upstream, no longer casting a shadow, and looked carefully around every rock, waiting immobile for likely
shapes to move. As the stream got deeper he had to
look for places to step, and as he did that, he saw a
flash of dull white five feet ahead of him. He froze,
stiffly, and let himself settle into a more comfortable
stance. He waited for what seemed a long time. He
sneaked a look at his watch. He was past his time limit.
He examined the stream carefully, made note of its

148

width, enough to stretch out in, the narrows around boulders, its depth, to his calves, the banks, some overgrowth, rocks, gravel in places, approachable on two sides, some sky overhead. He stepped backward, still looking, then sideways and on the bank. There he crouched and crept forward past the spot and peered from another angle. He could see them now, two trout about a foot long. They looked like grays. He waved his arm once and they flicked away downstream. He tried to follow on the bank but he had to favor each step and he didn't see them again. He got back in the stream, drank from it automatically, and hurried down to the lake wondering how he could catch fish without tackle. As soon as he was clear of the bush, he looked at the sky in all directions and listened. There was nothing.

He kept watching as he rubbed his feet dry and put his boots on once again. The trout only added to his frustration. He rolled down his pants, he felt ridiculous enough as it was, and remembering, stuffed the hanky in his pocket. The physical needs had begun to depress him. They were more than work, they were demands with threats behind them. Nature's blackmail. He gathered his bundles, looked as he walked, stopped and squatted to pick up the dried socks, and stumbled his way to the site, always watching, where the first thing he did was kick open the arrowhead.

"I'm back here!"

It was 5:17.

Angrily he cleared the ashes and thumped the stones back in place. The sudden rapid exertion left him trembling, and his anger ceased abruptly, on a note of warning, when he saw he needed firewood. It was too expensive an emotion. Chastened by his outburst he freed his heavy shirt and went south into the bush and pulled out dead branches and piled them there on the beach. He dragged over enough for the night, broke off what he'd need to start the fire right, and got things ready for supper. The water was last. Then he sat and waited, barefooted, and tried to contain his disappointment.

The sky stayed empty, except for a beautiful evening. He finished eating around seven-thirty, thin soup and all, and sat hunched and cross-legged for the first time in many years. Above the lake the sun and the few clouds were deepening into red and the beach in front of him was soft with backlit shapes. Birds seemed to be feeding everywhere, on bugs most likely. He took a cigarette from the pack, looked at it as something alien, and tossed it into the fire. Nineteen left. He remembered it was Sunday and wondered about God. They didn't come. He renewed the map and thought about the fish. There were stories about bare-handed fishing. There's still time.

"They might turn up."

He didn't believe it.

After sunset, while the light was still strong, he shifted the evergreen bedding closer to the fire and placed logs on each side to warn him if he rolled too far. He kept vigil again, just in case. There was only the moon, more crescent, setting later than the night before. And at late twilight he lay down, quite sensibly, and watched the sky darken around the first visible stars.

150

14

There was a brightness outside him, he knew that, but there were also trout in a stream and he was making impossible plans and saw pilots looking far below them and reporting negatives. They've told her by now, that's sure, and she's at Henri's listening to the search on his radio. Or maybe they had her stay in Montreal, it'd be better that way, and she could come out when there was definite news. Only there couldn't be any, not unless they found me, so they're hearing nothing and wondering. Tom and Nancy wouldn't want to stay home, they'd want to be with the action, and he'd be uptight and try to be casual, the old man'll be all right, he's pretty cool, and Nancy'd refuse to believe in disasters, Dad knows that plane too well. Yes, but maybe there was something wrong with it. No, not with the mechanics he's got: he's somewhere. Yeah, I'm somewhere. I'm right here. Tell 'em I like to explore. You know that. Tell them.

He opened his eyes to the brightness. It was everywhere and it kept going and he couldn't focus on it and suddenly he was aware of the morning sky. He sat up to confirm it, and everything else slipped back into place.

It was 5:20, just before sunrise. When he adjusted to being up and about, he was glad it was early. They wouldn't have gone back upstairs yet, and it delayed the anxiety of watching. He needed the time to do things.

He didn't wash. He set up fire and water for making breakfast, and in the cool dawn, with one boot wet, he began to collect firewood of all sorts and pile it just past the open arrowhead. He stopped to boil and eat the greens, and continued to work until the wood was over six feet high. By that time it was full morning, close to seven-thirty, and the sky had to be kept in contact. He set fire to the huge mound, waited till it was fully caught and heaped it with foliage and decayed wood and any debris that would make smoke. Dense black and gray clouds rose from it, and it seemed able to conjure anything. It would do his looking for him. He closed the arrowhead carefully, as though he were performing a rite, gathered his two shirts and walked where it pointed.

Along the way he looked for a long thin branch that could serve as a pole and, finding none, he set about laboriously cutting one from a small tree. He did it slowly and precisely, shaving whittles all around, not removing them, and doing it more deeply a second time.

"We'll get fish."

He snapped and sliced the branch free and carried it,

foliage and all, around the bay and to the pine tree. After gathering the leaves and greens he needed, he trimmed the branch so as to keep the three prongs at its fork and about five feet of handle. He studied it like a stymied golfer and watched the smoke and tried to imagine a design that would work. It was getting on, near nine-thirty. He concentrated on the problem, just to keep his mind busy. But worry tightened around him all the same. He decided to carve three barbs.

It couldn't be done. He found out on the first one. The barbs couldn't be small and strong at the same time, and a big one the size of his thumb was too stubby to work. He settled for three tapering points, shaved down to be roughly parallel, but the green wood was too pliable and he had to sharpen the prongs in their natural directions. Even then, when he had finished, he discovered that the points were soft. They'd never penetrate, especially underwater.

The smoke rose pleasantly over the site and signaled nobody. At one glance it was cozy, the hardy life, an advertiser's delight, at another it was ominous. He went back to it, going over the ridge and sliding down the slope, and the fire seemed to say that somebody was there, some lucky guy out camping, and it made him strangely aware of himself, a person to others. Hi. Hi. Nice day. Great. Catch anything? No, just a few bites. The banalities covered a profound dimension. He thrust the carved stick into the base of the fire and kept pulling it out to examine it. How'd'ya find this place? Oh, just an accident. When it was sufficiently charred he cooled it in the water and scraped it in the sand and recarved the points a little. They were much harder.

The sun made him look at the time. It was eleven. He put more debris on the fire and stared awhile at the sky with a resigned lack of expectation. The fire was doing the watching. You think they'll come? I dunno. They've had time by now. It's not a matter of time. He went back to the area near the pines, leaving the stick at the end of the bay, and foraged for greens and wild strawberries, lunch.

"What's it a matter of, then?"

He was speaking to no one in particular, merely a dimension who was answering like someone. Merely.

"It's a matter of chance, a lucky guess."

"They'll never guess."

"They might."

Speaking made the words seem rational. It brought consciousness to some other level and avoided the worry of silent thought. They might be dragging that lake just to make sure you didn't go down over there, and that takes time.

"Yeah."

He got to the stream around noon and he kept his boots on to scout it from the far bank, away from the sun, in case.

"It took you nearly seven hours to get here."

Almost a full day's work, nonstop. He was tired. He decided to keep going. He stayed just far enough to see the surface of the water and crept to the edge whenever he wanted a better look. The homemade spear felt like a sham, a kid pretending. He saw nothing in two direc-

154

tions. He tried it again in the water, barefooted and edging forward inch by inch. It took a long time both ways. He saw no fish.

"They come in here to feed."

"You sound like a guide conning the big sport."

"That's right."

He went lakeside to see the smoke still rising and returned a little upstream and sat down to watch for fish. He knew it was virtually impossible to spot them, but the rest was welcome and there was nothing else to do, except wonder about the worst.

"You're going to have to set a time limit."

They're going to. They'll have to. They can't search forever. They'll report that you disappeared without a trace and you're presumed dead.

"Not yet."

"Sooner or later."

"But not yet."

When he felt rested he examined the stream again, in vain, and checked the smoke, now thinning out. It became a routine, back and forth. Not dull, nor silly, or serious. He simply accepted it. Time lost much of its meaning. He noticed ferns, which could be edible, and mosses and elaborate mushrooms which he knew shouldn't be eaten, thanks to folklore and the mushroom industry, berries not to be tried and flowers like small orange trumpets pointing downward. At one point he relieved his bowels, using ferns, and washed his hands, downstream. And when he sat down again, unheedful, with nothing ready, he saw the white underside of a trout.

He ducked away from the bank, slipped off his boots, and groped for the carved stick. It was like panic. His heart thumped and he was breathing fast, and he had to stop to control himself. It was only a fish. Sure. He went in lakeside very deliberately, still excited, and crept upstream conscious of the glare of his feet. He moved flat-footed, not taking steps, just lifing his feet enough to clear bottom, and holding the stick upright in front of him like a low flag. He stopped often and long and decided to do nothing if the fish swam past him. He needed it stationary, and he needed it there. He wondered if the trout could hear his breathing and he almost gave himself an answer, out loud.

Painstakingly he inched forward some twenty feet, trying not to teeter and doing most of it by stopping. Stillness was more important than movement. All sorts of alternatives came to mind, damming the stream with stones, or logs, or sticks driven into the bottom, all heavy work, putting bugs on the water as bait, using his shirt as a net, boot laces as fishing line. And finally in the shallows ahead of him he saw the trout, then another. He became rigid.

By crouching slightly he managed to move forward without swaying. The effort made his whole body tremble, and he stopped to rest some four feet away from them. They were swimming in figure eights, perhaps suspicious, but they stayed in the area. He stood as still as he could, feet together, left hand supporting his right, waist high, hoping they'd think he was a tree. It wasn't going to be easy or fast. He tried to relax and get rid of the shakes. The fish didn't come near him.

He zigzagged his left foot away from him and shifted to a more comfortable position. It made further movement impossible, but moving was out of the question anyway. He waited. He had time to figure out what he'd do.

The fish seemed unconcerned. They swam around less and moved in a smaller area. Gradually he stooped forward, gripping the stick in both hands, and reached out to hover the points over the water. The fish were too far, and he couldn't wait long in that position. Then one of them moved, and toward him. He judged the distance, the angle, and decided. He plunged the stick straight down.

There was a great fuss. The bottom was immediately clouded. He couldn't see, but he could feel the stick holding something down, something that struggled and wiggled. He kept the stick tight with one hand and got out of the squat he was in. The water wasn't clearing, and he didn't know how the fish was caught. If it was just pressed down, he couldn't fling it to shore. He reached down and touched the fish. It struggled all the more. But he knew it was facing right. He turned to get behind it, reached in again, and dug his fingers into its gills and gripped hard. He pulled it out, dropped the stick, and hit it on the head, hard, backhand with his knuckles. In three blows it was stunned. There was no red on it, it was speckled, about a foot long. He went after the floating stick and got on the bank.

He was out of breath and sweating, and still trembling. He felt like crying. He held on to the trout until it stopped twitching, and placed it carefully away from the bank. He washed his hands off, and couldn't stop shaking. He went to get his boots, carried them back, and rubbed his feet dry. Something seemed to have gone wrong, he wasn't elated, he was exhausted. The bugs had bitten him badly. The omens were all negative.

His watch said 6:10. He couldn't believe it.

"It took all day."

There was still a little smoke from the signal fire. He put the trout with the broadleaves in his bush shirt, rinsed his hands again, and made his way back to the site. He stoked the signal fire and got the other going for supper and sat for a long while doing nothing. For the moment he was beyond hunger.

It was hard to sort things out. He began to realize that he'd hoped to catch the fish early and prepare it and eat it and then sit and watch the plane come in. Just like that. It was unrealistic. He had expended all his energy on that hope.

"I thought it'd be over by now."

"It's not."

"That's right. It's not."

"So?"

He didn't have an answer. At the lake he sliced through the underside of the trout, from gills to tail. It was a female. He ate the roe without a second thought, using the penknife to scoop it into his hand, and threw away only the intestines. He cleaned the forked stick he used for pushing stones and forced it, stomach side, through the fish's spine. He put the innards in its mouth. It wasn't the sort of thing he'd ever done on fishing trips, they kept only the fillets, for a frying pan, and butter, and spices, and wine if somebody brought some, a jump ahead of the store, that's all, you never left the kitchen. The trout looked as if it remembered being alive, it wasn't going to be a treat.

When the fire had coals he pushed the wood aside and held the fish over the heat. He was too tired to make a rig. He remembered to time it, five minutes on each side, and put it on a broadleaf to cool a little. He eased out the spine and flaked the meat in his fingers to avoid the bones. He ate everything he could, slowly and gratefully, without actually being conscious of enjoying it. He balked at the head and eyes, and placed the garbage on the beach. It might attract something. His first meal. He had no illusions about it. It might be his only one.

He followed it with the greens and the cooking water and got ready to watch the sun go down. The third day was already evening. He threw away another cigarette.

"They'll go by the number of passes, not by the number of days."

The idea circulated its images through his mind, planes and days and men at work. They've made a lot of passes, they could have covered that area by now depending on air speed and the size of the overlap at each pass. Search and Rescue would be ready to call it off.

"But not Martin. Not Betty."

He looked at all the distances, the lake disappearing to the southwest, the far shore with the hovering sun, the endless bush. The wilderness was becoming less temporary, less and less a place to wait in. The difference chilled him.

"There's tomorrow."

He scraped out a fresh triangle of relative positions and studied its hard simplicity. It held few alternatives.

"And then what?"

He didn't dare answer himself. To be sure was to be wrong, and hope has to be uncertain. There were clouds forming in the west, long heavy bands that were making the sunset earlier, and he wondered what he'd do if it rained.

15

He didn't really look at the time. It was enough to know it was early, and he wound his watch without taking it off. Morning had its meaning apart from time. The sky was thinly overcast, and through it the sun was a diffused red glare that was going to make everything hot. It hadn't rained. The air was damp and fresh, not cool enough to be chilly. It made his clothes smell wet, and his boots were actually covered with dew. The far shore of the lake wasn't there. It would clear. The day was simply here, as if he had continued yesterday into today. He felt as calm as the unmoving ground fog and he tried to think back over what might have gone through his head in the night. It could have been despair.

The two fires were cold ash and the tinder was a little clammy. It might have absorbed too much moisture. Another thing to look after, to remember. He spread it on the gravel for the sun. He organized wood for the bonfire and collected a pile for the signal. By then he was down to his T-shirt, it was routine. His hunger didn't surprise him or irritate him, nor his fatigue, it was all part of it, like urinating or looking to spot things or hear them. The fish bones were gone. There were no tracks, there wouldn't be on gravel. Do birds eat fish bones?

He continued the routine, in a way glad, despite the irony, to be doing it. It required no thinking. He gathered a supply of plants, getting his clothes soaked in the high grasses, looked in on the stream, saw nothing, and wandered back and changed the leaves in the water hole. When the sun broke through he lit the bonfire, aware of having to use the lighter, and later, after eating, when the sky was clearing he set the signal pile ablaze and made it smoke. The summons rose and vanished over the wilderness, it felt about as useful as shouting.

He watched it helplessly, a little afraid. He wasn't calm any more, his feelings were beginning to surface.

"Today."

He didn't know what he meant, hope, or doubt, or nothing. It must have been on his mind all night, and his thoughts were getting ready to buzz over it. Today was here. The tomorrow past which he hadn't dared look. He still couldn't do it.

He cleaned the points of the fishing stick, giving that his full attention, and went north to the far side of the stream and searched it, twice, for trout. There were none. And he had to sit, to wait, and let things happen. The noise of the water was disorienting, and the

162

woods, unheard, seemed more isolated. It made him cautious for no reason he could see, and fearful of nothing in particular. An enemy, man or animal, would be welcome. He grew more and more aware of himself as a presence, the only presence. He felt nameless. And nowhere.

"You're not really expecting anybody. Are you?"

"No, I'm not."

It seemed to explain a lot, the numbness, which looked calm at first, the negative feeling that something was over, that there was no longer a need for waiting, or hoping. And the fear.

"They won't come. They can't. Not here."

He couldn't stay sitting. He searched from the bank again, studying the shapes of the flow, something to do, on purpose, listening to the changing sounds of the water, less loud that way and a little more present to him. He had created a fact, another fiat, this time a nothing based on nothing. He saw no alternative, nothing couldn't reveal itself. The only thing that could reveal itself would be real, a plane in the sky coming down to see the smoke. And it wasn't there. He saw no fish, and he was loath to sit again. He took to covering a distance, then kneeling awhile, and moving on as the need arose. Another routine, useful subjectively, while he tried to accept his fact.

He felt he had betrayed himself by hoping, that he'd lost an advantage of sorts, lost time.

"You couldn't have done a thing. It took till now to . . ."

He saw the diminishing returns, the spent energy,

hard physical work repeated over and over again, the constant walking for things, the hunger.

". . . to know."

The morning yielded nothing. When the sun was high, and hot, he went to the bay and stripped and washed in the lake. He noticed the weight he'd lost, muscles visible and hard, a seeming fitness, the body feeding on itself. He scrubbed the bites in his hair and in his thickening whiskers, a relief, but his nakedness made him feel fragile in the vast lake and he hurried to rub his body dry and get dressed. Just himself, and the smoke down the shore. Everything had changed, and the difference was absolute.

From the end of the bay he went to the clearing past the pines, conscious of the animal pace of his walking, the never even ground, and picked a firm handful of plants. With these he returned to the stream and ate them raw as he continued to watch. Everything seemed to press on him, there was no release at all from the hardness of nature, no place to retire to, and sigh, and have it over, even for a while, and no one to help provide it, to take on part of his consciousness. No one. Another person. Like himself. The idea was awesome. Rather than sit he went again to collect plants, and returned, and made that his routine, back and forth in long intervals, checking the sky at times, and storing what he gathered. His thoughts were always there. And he saw no fish.

The day passed into late afternoon. It was slowly confirming his fiat. It deepened his isolation, and hinted, weakly, of shifting hope into tomorrow. He didn't want more illusions. He made one last search of the stream and started back to the site with the collected greens. There were no planes.

The signal fire was a smoldering pile of ashes. He poked it open to preserve the embers and used them to light the cooking fire. He got everything ready and waited for the stones to heat. There was nothing left to do, the routine was over, it was time to attend to his thoughts. But his words came first.

"You can't stay here."

It was simple, in a way. It crystallized it all. He'd have to go. There was no sense debating it, it was only a matter of deciding. A mere act of will, sheer will. Where?

"South, walking."

"It's too far, it'd take . . . They can go a lot faster."

"Yeah, but they don't know where to go, you do."

"South."

He sat still for a long time, confronting the idea. And as he ate he found himself thinking of the site as a camp. It had facilities, of sorts. But he'd be leaving, the decision was taken. He had to get closer to the line of search, some seventy miles closer. He didn't want to dwell on the hazards, he knew them, or calculate the risks. He'd need hope of another kind now. Fear, and reason, could destroy it. Tomorrow.

"Tomorrow."

16

He was up before dawn. The early light was only beginning to give color to things, and he set about working quietly, keeping ahead of the arriving day. He rekindled the fire, which he'd stoked all night, and carried water from the lake. It was the last of that routine. He dried his boot with the heavy shirt, something he hadn't thought of before, and while the stones were getting hot he took the evergreen sprigs, bed and cushion, and spread them on top of the three signal piles he'd built three days ago. He did it with a certain elaboration, a gesture, like a priestly rite. It was all there was to breaking camp.

He ate as the sun was rising behind him, and watched the far shore receive its light. He left things as they were, the fire that would go out, the ashes, the eating sticks, the stones in the leaved hole, the meridian markers, the two lines of logs that had been the lean-to—signs of human presence. There were a lot of ashes. He'd been there a long time.

The preparations were few. The sunglass case he filled tight with tinder and slipped it on his belt. The check list, motel receipt, gasoline charge-slip he shoved with the money in his wallet and put it in his left hip pocket. In the right went the leather key case, coins, the small bottle opener, the comb, the hanky. He isolated the lighter and the penknife in his right side pocket and clipped the ball-point along the inside. The cigarettes were in his light shirt, buttoned down, the watch on his wrist, the greens bundled in the heavy shirt. His left pocket was free, as planned, and in it he stuffed as much tinder as was feasible. The fishing stick he'd carry.

At the end of the line of logs he made a final arrowhead pointing south. Then he took a brand from the cooking fire and lit the three signal piles. He watched them catch and smoke, and threw the brand on the last one. That was everything. It was time.

He began to move, south.

It didn't feel like departure. There was no moment to it, he was just walking. Going. In a hundred feet he was passing his entrance into the bush, an opening scarred and littered with his work, and he moved on, picking his way among the small boulders, noticing everything, the tough shrubs, the changing trees, birds scolding him out of their area, possible far-off landmarks to aim at later. Eventually he reached the rocky point of his first day's exploration. A mile. He looked back and saw the smoke. It was thin and wispy in the distance.

He went round the point, which shut him off from the site, and came to the brook where he had first been afraid to drink. He stopped and drank willingly this time, and searched a length of it for fish. He saw none. And when he emerged and resumed his walking, it struck him that he had passed into unfamiliar country. Everything ahead of him was new, and it looked like a vast nowhere. On his left was the rest of the clearing, the part he hadn't penetrated, full of shrubs and tall weeds. It became thick bush in about a quarter mile. The rock-strewn beach meandered in and out of sight, probably not beach in places, and it enclosed water whose end he couldn't see. The sun, two hours up, somewhere just past east, his left, looked strange and steady, revealing unknown places and imperceptibly lifting shadows from the countryside. He regarded it with felt respect. Only direction gave meaning to the wilderness. South. And only the sun gave him that.

There was no rhythm to his walking, the ground was too rough, and he couldn't maintain a regular pace, however slow. He had to wind his way through the scattered rock and meander with the weaving shoreline, heading a little west of south. He sought out natural paths and clearings and fixed on bigger rocks and clumps of growth, arriving at them so gradually they looked familiar when he got there, and forgetting them, forever, as he passed. The sameness of rock and gravel and water, and the slow crunching of his steps, lulled him into a physical monotony. His eyes and feet were doing the work, and his mind was free, or at least unused. Even worry seemed impossible. But it was there, it accompanied his hunger.

As the morning grew hotter he had to stop more often to rest. He eventually took off his light shirt and arranged the hanky on his head. The bundle of greens, in two shirts, got awkward and sweaty, it was like carrying laundry, the fishing stick was cumbersome, his hands weren't free, and the stuff in his pockets made his pants cling to him. He kept moving as he thought of it, and finally hit upon an answer. He tucked the tails of the shirt in the back of his belt, sat down, spread the shirt behind him, maneuvered the bundle onto it, and made a flap by tying the sleeves in front of him. It worked fairly well, and at the rate he had to go it didn't interfere with his walking. He couldn't help being aware of the pouch hanging over his buttocks, the knotted hanky sticking out like curlers, a six-day growth on his face, and the strange trident that wasn't even a walking stick. It just missed being funny. Necessity made the absurd practical.

Around noon, clock time, when the sun was high and almost in front of him, he began to look for shade to rest in and stopped whenever he saw a likely opening in the bush. It was slow progress. He negotiated some greens out of the makeshift pouch and ate them little by little, it was pointless to actually stop as though for lunch. His sorties into the sun grew shorter. And at real noon, one o'clock daylight-saving, he put his watch back to twelve, standard time, and pointed the hour hand at the sun. Twelve was south. It'd make things easier to calculate. He had a 360° object that could count hours precisely, and he felt there was a way of making it serve as a compass. He set the problem aside until he had more data, he'd have to see how the sun behaved relative to the watch.

It gave him something to relieve the monotony. He

kept walking, and resting, and brushing bugs away, and mulling over the problem. At one o'clock by the new setting he pointed the 1 hand to the sun and tried to see if twelve was south. It didn't seem right. The angle made by the five-minute markings was too small to be sure of anything. He kept going. He still couldn't make out the end of the lake, but he'd learned to read the shoreline better. Well ahead of him a point of land seemed to reach too far into the lake, and he guessed it might be a bay. Gradually as he approached, the point acquired perspective and separated into the near and far sides of an inlet. It didn't mean anything beyond being a discovery, and in a sense everything was that. At two o'clock he pointed the 2 hand to the sun: the twelve mark still wasn't pointing south, it seemed east of it. He'd need a bigger angle. But a bigger angle would be three o'clock, 90° away from twelve, which would represent west, and west was really six hours from noon, not three. Something was wrong with his figuring. Twelve wasn't south, except at noon.

Again he put the problem aside. He was entering the inlet. Its sides, some hundred yards across, were a mix-up of brush and clearings, hardly any beach, none in spots, with heavy shrubs hanging over the water, and low dense growth and dead broken trees in the rising background. He waded around the overhangs. The water was shallow and clear, though the place reminded him of a swamp. The bugs were thicker. Near midway he came to a clearing with shrubs high enough to give shade and with a wide-mouthed creek that narrowed inland and seemed hardly to be flowing. He drank from it as he crossed to get to the shade and stopped to rest and reconsider his problem. There was a connection between the sun's movement and clock time, and he had to find it while he could still use the lake to verify a south-by-west direction. He looked at the watch, not seeing the hour and trying to understand what it did. It completed its circle, 360°, in twelve hours, and the sun did *its* circle in twenty-four. The hour hand was twice as fast as the sun. It was a clue, a basis for an exact link, but before he could pursue it he saw movement in the creek. He freed himself of his baggage, save the stick, recrossed the creek by wading in the lake, to approach without casting shadows, and crept inland a little as he peered in the water. There was nothing. Then he waved an arm and saw movement: minnows darting like sudden ripples. The stick was useless.

He sat on one haunch, limp with disappointment, and fatigue, and watched them with growing despair. Nature seemed to thwart him at every turn. He resented his hunger and the heat and the frustrating minnows. A small thing, seeing minnows instead of trout, big laughs on a fishing trip, but it triggered emotions the long walk had kept down and it made him feel helpless and afraid. Physically helpless. A feeling that invoked disaster. To walk away would be to enter a state of mind that could become permanent.

"You can't pass it up. It's now."

He returned to his baggage, again by the lake, going slowly, deliberately not hurrying or fussing. He could afford to fail, what he couldn't afford was not trying.

He twisted and cut off a thin branch to match his fishing stick, and with these he experimented awhile with his light shirt until he fashioned a crude net: sticks through the sleeves, collar and yoke downward facing out, the tails and sleeves gripped part way down around the sticks to allow him to maneuver the device. He placed it by the lake and went upstream to the narrows and blocked them off as best he could with rocks. Then in bare feet, with pants rolled, he proceeded quietly upstream, holding the net in front of him. He scared the minnows inland, and when he reached the narrows he put the net in the water, waited to let things settle, and inched ahead toward the blocking rocks.

The shirt resisted the water and billowed when he pushed it. The minnows would be swept out of it if he jerked it up. He maneuvered it under them, let them get used to it, and raised it gently and slowly, and finally when they felt it and scurried he closed the sticks together, held that with one hand, grabbed the collar with the other, and hauled everything to the side.

He let the water run out and looked at his catch. He had about a dozen minnows. Again without hurrying he went round to his boots, put the minnows in one of them, added a little water, and repeated the entire netting procedure. He caught fewer the second time, and none the third. He poured them all on the shirt and examined a few for sharp bones and rough fins. Then he ate them raw and wiggling, one by one, and had to hold down his disgust. By the time he was finished he was partly used to it.

He didn't wait for things to dry. He reorganized his

baggage, worked his way to the end of the inlet where the beach widened, and resumed his walking. The sun was noticeably to his right, past four by his watch. He paused to study the dial.

With the hour hand to the sun, the twelve mark was well east of south, and south seemed to be near the two-o'clock mark. He imagined the sun's circle, the watch's circle, and thought of them as degrees, not time. The sun moved 15° an hour, the hour hand moved 30° an hour, twice as much, always twice as much. So when the watch showed two hours past noon, the hand had moved 60° while the sun had moved only 30°. So if you want to keep the twelve mark as south, you don't point the hour hand to the sun, you point a mark halfway between twelve and the hour hand. He tried it. He pointed the two mark to the sun, and saw that twelve pointed south.

The system worked, but it seemed unnecessarily complicated, and to be exact he'd have to do it on the hour. He puzzled over it as he walked, and he realized he was still assuming that the twelve mark had to be south. Noon was south, not twelve, because the sun on the meridian made it noon. It was purely arbitrary that the top of the watch had the number twelve on it. What counted was the hour hand.

"Okay, so use that."

Then he knew he had the question right: with the hour hand pointing to the sun, where's south? He positioned the watch again. South was halfway between the hour hand and the twelve mark. It would always be that way no matter what time it was, the relationship was absolute. He had his compass. He almost quickened his pace.

He kept checking his discovery and it kept on being right. He was fascinated in a detached way, and he let it occupy him fully. It gave him a task when he stopped to rest, and something to look forward to as he walked. He marveled at the precision of the watch, and more so at the unnoticeable movement of the sun. The earth rotating. It seemed fitting that the watch was dependent upon it, obeyed it somehow, just as he did. It put things right side up.

At five, south was still there, and he thought the distant water a little west of it had an unbroken rim of trees. It was hard to be sure. An abrupt narrowing would look that way, or a series of bays and points, or a sharp turn of the lake. He gave that his attention, tempted to make a long final effort to get there, but he stopped and rested as usual. There was no "there" to get to. It would simply be another new place, in transit, and it too would take its measure of work. The rim didn't separate as he approached and the far shore got closer. At six he could see it clear and uniform, but he halted to look at his watch: six was the sun, dead west, twelve was east, 180° in a straight line, and three was south. A nice fit. Near six-thirty he reached the end of the lake.

It was simply more shore. It narrowed into a long uneven U-turn and had no outlets that he could see, just a place without another side. There was beach, some twenty feet wide, more in places, and ragged shrubs where the woods began. He picked one of the

174

wider sections and put his things down. Along the edge of the woods he found the right flat-leaved evergreens, broke off enough boughs to sleep on, made them up in the middle of the beach, and returned for wood and twigs and tinder and arranged these lakeside of the bedding. He made a reserve pile a few feet away and finally sat down. Camp. The full respite made him feel his exhaustion. He was weak and shaky, not far from tears, and he knew he had come too far in one day. Another lesson, late.

He stared at the distance he had traveled. The lake was darkening in the setting sun, and the long shores, going east of north, became a small gap on the horizon. It had looked fifteen miles long from the air and the site may have been five miles in. A ten-mile advance. It would be less from now on, it would have to be, in the bush, and he'd have nothing to reckon it with. He ate the last of the greens, raw and wilted, and after the sun went down he lit the fire with one careful stroke of the lighter. He made it smoke a little and dressed fully to keep the bugs from biting him too badly. Then he stretched out on the boughs and faced the sky and the growing moon and listened to the evening's noises. He was there. The fact seemed to be enough. He could make no plans, take no real thought for the morrow. And fear was as natural and chronic as hunger.

He remembered to take a cigarette from the pack. He threw it away from him toward the fire. Counting days was a sign of hope, in a way.

He was asleep before nightfall.

17

The day came to him slowly, like a puzzle, the early light impinging on his eyelids, the unevenness of the boughs under him, the fact of having all his clothes on, the chilly air, tight itchy lumps where his skin showed, and finally the sky, brighter toward the east and red with cloud, and with that the knowledge of where he was and what it meant. He sat up and then got up and he was ready to leave, for there was nothing to be done in the place, it was only where he had spent the night. The time said the sun had risen, but he couldn't see it yet, it hadn't cleared the forest on its side. In the bush he wouldn't see it at all. He'd have to wait.

He wound his watch carefully, stopping by guess before the spring was fully tight. He picked a spot to urinate and noticed that the lake had rises everywhere and saw hordes of birds fluttering at random and bickering over everything. He took the watch off to wash and drink water from the lake. His hands and forehead were bumpy and bleeding from insect bites, and his legs ached with incipient cramps. Hunger twisted his stomach and threatened not to let go. It made him feel light and stringy as if he could run as forgetfully as a child, but he knew the next phase would be tremors and muscles that felt like nerves. He searched the edge of the woods for edibles and found what looked like chokecherries with soft cores, which he didn't dare eat, and saw nothing else he wanted to try. He waited. He made no fire, and no signal. It would be evident that he'd been there. Or someone had. If someone were ever to see.

When the sun was higher, at six, dead east, he went into the bush to see if he could orient the watch. The trees were too dense, and the lowest sky he could see was in patches almost overhead. It would take hours for the sun to get there. Wasted hours. He came back to the beach, noticing how much cooler the woods had been, and picked up the fishing stick, still ready to go. The lake, and the end of it, held him. It was so definite a landmark, a real place, it allowed departure and return, and finding yourself. He had survived its waters, and six days along its shores. The bush was chaos next to it.

"I know you."

His voiced words bestowed a presence on the lake, and acknowledged it, as if he too were known. He didn't think it strange. It stirred him like a dream, a fearfulness that was not fear, and a gratitude, so it felt, or surprise, at having come this far. He could take nothing for granted, except presence.

177

"Yeah."

He turned his back on it, aware, and entered the bush.

It was thick. Low-branched evergreens grew into one another in most places and interrupted any natural paths. Some formed complete barriers, and others, older and higher, made waist-high tunnels that looked like dead ends. The ground was soft with decayed vegetation, almost hidden by short new growth, some of it little trees, and beneath that, when he scuffed it aside, was a black damp humus on which it all thrived. The air was heavy and cool. He could hear birds, by chirp and flutter, but he wasn't able to see any. The smell of the evergreens sharpened his hunger. A place for rabbits, he knew from sports talk, but he'd need a small-caliber rifle and a fresh snowfall to track them by, and snaring would take days, if he had a snare. He looked for the sun, in vain, and looked at his watch. He couldn't set a course, and if set, he couldn't hold it.

"It doesn't matter, you won't travel straight anyway."

He moved back and forth inside the edge of the woods, parallel—he thought—to the end of the lake, looking south for any sort of landmark, a tall tree, a hill, a break, but all he could see was the spaces between trees. He finally picked one and followed it, and turned into another, and another, left and right, detouring in and out of a random maze. He tried to remember what he had done, how far right, how far left, in order to compensate for each turn and stay on a generalized course. But it couldn't be done. There were too many turns, and he couldn't measure them, it would take a compass. He never knew where he was facing. Ahead was in front of him, and that was anywhere he happened to be looking. He knew from his first day's exploration around the site that he tended to circle to his right, and for a while he tried to keep bearing left, impossibly, for the terrain gave him few choices. He wandered deeper and deeper into the bush, guided only by the feeling of going forward, and in a half hour he knew he couldn't get back to the lake, he didn't know where it was. He was on his way, as decided.

He was careful about the twistings he had to make and he didn't stop to explore, for fear he'd become confused. He'd look for food later. His head felt locked into a forward position and he moved in a semi-crouch, peering through branches like a man who didn't want to be seen. As long as he concentrated on finding his way he had the illusion of having a section of trees ahead of him which became a section of trees behind him. It felt like progress, and he imagined it to be ultimately straight. Statistics leveling off. But more and more he felt it couldn't be so. The imposed illusion became a strain as he tried to maintain it, and the fear of turning his head made a menace of everything outside his line of vision. He began to sense that what he was going by wasn't really there. It was a thing in his head, the locked-in line of travel, an imaginary geometry, the terror of doing without it, of having nothing at all to go by.

"I'm doing it wrong."

"Well, stop. Just stop."

He came to a halt in a small clearing of bigger trees and stood facing forward. He still felt certain he was looking in the right direction, and he knew just as certainly that he wasn't. Certitude was unsuspected treachery. But he couldn't let go.

He kicked out a rut from the black humus to mark his assumed direction, and on that he placed a few dead branches to be able to see it from a distance. It served no real purpose except to anchor his lostness, but it freed him to move about. He circled the branches to see them from all sides, and their shapes changed and became more and more ambiguous until he returned to his original position and even then he was still in doubt until he examined the rut.

At the relatively correct end of the rut he gouged out an arrowhead, it felt as meaningless as writing on water. He stepped away from it, and he circled it again, this time looking outward into the changing forest. At every move his disorientation was sudden and complete. Everywhere he looked he saw the same new thing, solid trees for an instant forming real directions to be altered in the instant by the shift of his eyes or the motion of his body. It takes two points to make a line, and he had only one, himself, and that kept moving. He was a center, everywhere, in fact centers, an infinity of them.

He searched carefully for the sun. He turned slowly in a full circle, trying to see past the trees a little above eye level, hoping to catch a sparkle too bright to look at. There were only the tall crowded evergreens at the edge of the small clearing, thick and deep with shadow, their bases hidden in their own darkness. He shifted position and turned completely once more, and moved again and looked again. He saw only the forest, and a uniformly bright sky overhead. For a moment he longed for the lake and its certainties: water, and landmarks, and food such as it was, and knowing where south was, and . . . nothing else, it wasn't enough, it had been a closed system, a self-contained illusion, a routine that would be deadly in the long run. Like life.

"Life?"

Yes, life. That's what brought you here in the first place.

"Yeah, I guess it did."

He shook off the idea and looked up at the sky.

"It'll come up, it has to."

There at least was a certainty, a real one.

He took note of the crude landmark he'd made and walked in the direction it pointed until he reached the edge of the woods, a distance not more than fifty feet. There he turned left by arbitrary choice and began to examine the clearing. The method was meaningless, but it cut down on the chaos before him and it gave him the feeling of knowing where he was. The ground was uneven, clumpy, tangled with short wild growth, low bushes, tiny flowers, what looked like thick pads of blackish green, mosses most likely, and fernlike plants and spindly new evergreens that seemed to be surprised they were there. He went slowly, not to disturb the bugs, or get overheated and attract them. He saw none of the plants he'd come to know at the campsite. The thought of them made his mouth ache, and his hunger seemed to send pains into his legs. He tightened his belt without thinking and wondered what plants he could eat. He stopped long and often over the idea and did nothing. At one point he realized that he'd lost his imagined fix on the marker and he couldn't know how much of the clearing he'd covered. It struck him as odd that he'd lose his bearings in an area the size of his back yard. Fifty feet across. The place smelled like air freshener, like an aerosol can in the bathroom, instant nature where there could be none, the fakery of civilization, the real thing evoked metaphors of the phony, it seemed funny in a remote way. Surveyors had pinpointed that back yard, and builders, and laws, and contracts, and money for the house in front of it, and bought grass, and an ornamental fence that looked like natural wood, and neighbors who'd done the same thing. No way to get lost there, you stayed found forever, in somebody's computer. Spence. Spence, what . . .? It's all right, I'm spraying the back yard, with pine. Betty would laugh at that. Betty.

"If I don't make it, I want you to know . . ."

He fell silent, and made no attempt to evade his awareness. If I don't make it. Existence had become sharply evident.

In the next moment, without thinking or even deciding, he broke off a few ferns at their base and began eating them in small bites. For some reason they made him salivate heavily, and he wondered what he'd do for water. One worry at a time was enough. He was trusting to the plants, he'd have to trust to luck for anything else. There was really nothing to figure out, nothing to do except take chances. The very logic of it frightened him. He put the fishing stick through his belt to have both hands free, and browsed from plant to plant like an animal, except for his fear, and gradually his hunger became less intolerable.

He noticed everything on the ground, a profusion of growth that left no earth to be seen. He found younger ferns, which tasted better, and kept moving in response to his random discoveries. From time to time he looked, in vain, for his marker, and he wondered why he felt he had to return to it. It would tell him where he'd come from, where he'd entered the clearing, no more, and even that wasn't important, he was already where he was. Yet he knew that if he started looking for the marker, it would become obsessive: a need for continuity perhaps, another illusion, thinking in terms of maps, there are no blanks on a good map, you fill everything in, even if you're wrong. The matter left him slowly, and as he got used to the area, it seemed more and more real and not something he was lost in. He tried to see it as itself, looking at it without ulterior purpose, and he had the fleeting realization that it was a place simply because he was there, because he had made it into one by his presence. There seemed to be more to the idea, but it vanished as soon as he was aware of it. It wasn't a place he was looking for, it was a direction.

And he had that at his next turn. He saw a bright flash through the trees and tested it and almost rejoiced when it wouldn't go away. It was 8:25. He pointed the hour hand at the flashing trees and picked up south halfway to noon, some 60°, the sun at his left.

It made him reorient himself. The clearing fell into place as a definite locale, like a merry-go-round that had just stopped. South was on the "other" side where, he presumed, he had not been. The whole area seemed smaller, a piece of ground that could be crossed in a minute now that he knew which way to go. He took his time adjusting to the new dimensions. The sun would keep moving upward and sideways, fifteen degrees an hour, one degree in four minutes, southeast at nine o'clock. He'd need it high in the bush. Next time he'd wait for it before moving. Next time.

"That'll be tomorrow."

And the sun will decide even that. Another presence.

He went south across the clearing. And as he got close to the edge of it, the sun disappeared behind the dense trees. He backed away to see it again, made sure of his line of travel, and picked the least crowded opening into the bush and went in. The terrain took him on a haphazard course. He moved a few steps at a time, stopped to hunt for a way through, and calculated a possible return to his imagined route. It was tedious and impractical among the random trees, a dead reckoning that needed compass and paper and landmarks. He abandoned the idea of any system and simply moved on, looking for the sun and trusting to an instinct he knew didn't exist. After a long while the terrain began to slope downward and the ground became damp and then wet and the trees thickened like shrubbery. He had to push his way through the tangled

184

branches. He did it slowly and grimly, stopping after each effort, aware that he could be going in circles in this morass. He tried to favor a tendency to the left, even to avoiding openings on his right, but it was all he could do to keep from meandering too widely. There was still no sun. He should have waited, it was the only way to gain time and distance. And strength. He decided to stop.

He couldn't sit on the wet ground and he couldn't lean on the bushy trees. He squatted from time to time and stood around looking and wondering. He idled his way into adjacent areas, and soon he was going very slowly from place to place like a man inspecting a garden. It was easier than standing still. Gradually he noticed that the ground was less soggy. And at every long while it got firmer and firmer. The trees thinned out a little and he was able to make out the slope of the ground, a slight incline, upward. It was as good as a compass reading. He followed it laboriously, losing and finding it through the brush, and finally with a suddenness that surprised him, he was aware all at once of fewer low-branched evergreens, of birches and other trees with high bare trunks, and the morning sun behind them scattering light patches on the forest floor. He crested the incline and sat on the ground to ease his trembling legs. The real day was beginning, here. And he was exhausted.

"You must have covered a mile."

"Yeah, the hard way."

"I did it all wrong."

The woods said nothing about how far they went. At

most he could see some two hundred feet into them. It was probably less, it was difficult to tell distances. The trees varied in size and hid behind each other on different planes and took shape and depth from the southeast light.

"You can do the next one right. It'll be easier."

When his legs stopped shaking, a little past nine-thirty, he set a course to the right of the sun and moved on. He felt almost free after the struggle with the evergreens. The ground was strewn with debris, and he had to step over things rather than walk, but he could see ahead of him and stay on a rough course and merely dodge trees instead of making wide blind detours around them.

His sense of progress cheered him for a while, but before long the contrast wore off and he was left with nothing but the new terrain. The woods and the sunlight began to seem permanent, and his pace soon became a constant trudging. He couldn't determine how far he'd come or how much farther he'd have to go. He'd need a map for that. Or a road. He'd see the ground only once, and that wasn't enough. He was one day away from the site to the north, a place he could never find again, and maybe twenty from where south would end. No, not days, suns. Days were irrelevant without the sun. He felt he was moving in an unchanging present. The same ahead as behind. A repeated now. He wasn't used to it. His mind clamored for reference points, a chart where all the lines met all the lines, a future, not sheer timeless motion. He'd had that when he thought he was drowning. Now is outside of time.

"It's like death."

"Yeah. It is."

He tried to find a system that would give him the shortest route and he had to keep stopping and lining up the watch. All he got was an imaginary line that wouldn't stay still. Everything that mattered moved: the sun, the hour hand, the wrist that had the watch, himself, the trees that changed angle as he did. It was no use. The best he could do was keep the sun in front of him, less and less on the left. It was a lot easier and it saved time. He pressed himself to keep going, straight lines or no, and rested according to a crude schedule, some ten minutes for a half hour's work, and took readings which were more and more unnecessary. The woods didn't change much. Now and then the trees got sparser and bigger in areas that looked like neglected parks, and the ground rose gently over long distances. He timed his rests so that he was walking at noon when the sun was high in the south. It didn't seem to make much difference, except that he knew for a few minutes how erratic his course actually was. His pace had slackened. Hunger was now a chronic pain and his thirst kept reminding him he had no water. He wondered when the woods would end. Flying over them you see nothing but bush. And lakes.

The woods persisted. Near two o'clock he noticed he was on higher ground that sloped across his path and upward to his left. The trees thinned out as they rose and he could make out a few pines above him. He was on the side of a hill. Or a ridge. He planned a detour carefully. He piled deadwood on the crotches of a small birch until it looked like no other tree, then deciding he would be climbing east he first looked west to see what it would be like on returning, did an about turn and started uphill slowly. Every so often he placed markers in the trees and made sure he'd be able to see them on the way back. It was work, and again he wondered why he was doing it. A precaution. A ritual to dispel uncertainty. Returning would be returning to nowhere.

The top of the rise turned out to be a small plateau. It was sparsely furnished with trees, mainly pines of the sort he'd seen at the site, and it extended a few acres on all sides before beginning to dip back into the forest. He stayed in the unobstructed sun and tried, between trees, to make out the countryside below him. He was too low for a complete view, and the corridors he did see made the bush look infinite. The ground was covered by shrubs and grasses and small plants, some with flowers, others with green berries. He broke off young leaves indiscriminately, tasted them, and ate only the ones that were mild. It didn't help much, but it seemed to deceive his stomach. He took the awkward stick from his belt and stretched out in the tall grass, oblivious to insects, and hoped his fatigue would seep into the ground. The sky was a relief, it was always familiar somehow, a hint of home, like resting on a Saturday afternoon. A place to spend the night. High and dry. No, not without water, and not while there was still sun to travel by.

He kept noticing the biggest pine tree. It was old and unkempt, with a dark broken bark like tough old shingles that had lost their shapes. It was close to two feet wide, its bottom branches thick and dead, and it looked as high as two houses, five, six stories, sixty feet, or more. A height to see from. If there was anything to see. He waited, to let his hopes subside and to let the idea become practical. Then he went to it.

The lowest branch was slightly above his head, and from there the others wound upward around the trunk. Easy for a boy, or an athlete, grinning over a cereal box. He thought about it. He took off his bush shirt and his boots and socks, he'd be more careful that way and have less weight to lift and he'd feel the branches better. He put his arms around the branch, the trunk behind him, and swung his legs over it and tried to roll himself topside. He couldn't do it, the second time even less. He let himself down and thought about it again.

The next highest branch was to the left of the lowest and just out of reach. Facing the trunk, he practiced once, jumping, to see if he could secure a hold on it, rested, then leaped up, caught the branch, pushed with his feet on the trunk and managed to get one foot on the lower branch. With that leverage and by twisting clear of the branch he was holding he pushed himself upright between the upper branches. All his strength seemed gone. He rested again, making sure he wouldn't slip as he relaxed, and looked for spaces to continue the ascent. In a while, one branch at a time, testing and careful not to strain, he went as high as he thought safe, and turned to find the sun.

The whole countryside was forest. From below him where each tree was distinguishable it advanced and thickened and foreshortened itself into an enormous and undulating green mass that continued, he estimated, for at least ten miles to the horizon. Here and there it blackened and lightened as the shadows or vegetation changed, and past a certain distance everything looked the same, a uniform dark tone that he knew to be really green. Far off nothing moved. No birds. No smoke. No airplanes.

Beginning close by and allowing for his oblique angle of vision he examined the bush carefully in an effort to get used to distances. Where he could still make things out reasonably well he tried keeping them in view in a sort of circular plane. He propped himself in the tree and cupped his hands over his eyes like binoculars to keep concentrated on small areas. Gradually he grew able to read the bush a little. At a half mile, as he thought, gaps were still visible, and at a mile things were very foreshortened. Size diminished and density increased. But he was able to compare masses in one area, one behind the other, a sudden ridge of greater density on the far side. It meant a space of some sort, a big one, or a depression. He stared at it and uncupped his hands one by one. It was still there. He looked around it and away from it, and was able to find it again. Two or three miles away. He couldn't be sure.

Getting a fix on it was difficult. Only by stretching his left arm could he get his watch in the sunlight and that put it too far to use. And if he changed position he was afraid he might lose his target completely. He pointed at it and held his arm stiff as he looked up to

see where he could go. Satisfied that he could climb by
feel, he kept his eyes on the far-off area and slowly
pushed himself up with his legs. He was able to lean
his left arm on a branch and have the sunlight strike
the watch. He lost the target and found it again and
took a lot of trouble to position himself right. The sun
was close to three o'clock, southwest, and the area,
when he found it once more, was close to two, 30°
southwest of south.

Relieved and tired, he made his way down. The area
had disappeared from view. It was a memory now, an
angle that would keep changing. Four and a half hours
to sunset, two or three before the sun was hidden by
the bush, two in thick woods, three and more if they
were thin enough to let him see the red sky. He sat and
looked at the formidable direction he'd have to take.
He put on socks and boots and tried to decide on
whether to stay or go.

"With luck a mile an hour."

"Make it a half mile."

By sunset. If there was something there. And if he
didn't lose the way.

He got ready, the long stick through his belt, the
bush shirt on his arm. He stuffed the pocket with fresh
leaves, checked the direction, and went downhill into
the woods. He felt flimsy and unreal compared to the
vastness he was entering, but he was entering it anyway. It was a new feeling, more subtle than disguised
panic, a sort of self-abandonment that wasn't yet reckless. He felt strangely at peace with it. It simplified

things to one factor: the limits of his own endurance. That, at least, he could come to know. It would be unmistakable.

The sun was lower than he had anticipated. It followed him through the trees, blinking and glaring behind the leaves and branches, and making deeper shadows in the cooling woods. He kept it more and more to his right, hoping to tend south and approach the area broadside. The woods set the pace, an unhurried weaving that couldn't be timed or measured and that had to continue over a distance that would never be known. He accepted it and finally took it for granted and bothered only with direction and the terrain immediately in front of him. The bugs made him put on his bush shirt. His rests were short and frequent, and he used them to take bearings that got more difficult to estimate. In time, well past four, he began to notice that the floor had less undergrowth in places. In others it was packed down in what seemed like meanders. The more he looked the more apparent they became and at length he realized what they must be: animal trails. Big animals, like deer or moose.

The tracks had tended downhill and roughly on his course, which meant he had kept crossing the same one. He decided to see what direction it took. He set up a marker with branches, knowing he could back-trail to it, took bearings, and started following the tracks. He checked the trail against the sun at every turn. And as he lost his distrust the going got better. He didn't have to find his way or decide on short routes around the trees. The obstacles were fewer and clearer on the trodden ground and the windings seemed to contour themselves into a downward slope. The lowland was what he wanted. The sun remained generally to his right, at times almost in front of him, and never completely outside his peripheral vision. It was always there and it made the trail more and more welcome. In time he stopped taking bearings. The watch served little purpose now, the problem was where and when.

Near six he felt that too much time had gone by. The day's trek would have to stop. The sun was low in the west. In an hour and a half it would be gone. The woods would get dark quickly. And he knew he should be getting ready for the night. Three hours' travel. He was sure he had made two miles, possibly three. And in the right direction, mainly. But he had nothing except the trail and the knowledge that he had drifted along somewhere between south and southwest. A big margin for error.

"You must have passed it."

Maybe not.

"I don't even know how far it was."

He tried to remember what the land had looked like from the pine tree and whether he could have gone too far south. The effort confused him, and he had to force himself to be calm.

"If I could see it, it was close enough. Two miles."

He decided to gamble.

"Go dead west."

He left the trail and made his way toward the sun. He hadn't gone far when he realized that he shouldn't be seeing it at all if the woods were continuous. And with that he saw glare from the ground ahead, and pushed on to see a narrow lake in front of him. He emerged into the still warm sun. Water. The animals knew where to find it.

He just stood and looked at it, immensely relieved, weak and tired, his whole body trembling, even his voice. The biggest problem remained.

"Food."

18

He had fire, and wood, smoke to keep some of the bugs away, and boughs to sleep on. The routine was like a gift, it was measured against nothing. He had the forest to listen to, a night that wasn't silent or fully dark, stars to look at. Water to drink. The feel of stubble on his face, muscles aching like bruises, bites that never stopped itching, and pain inside, as much a part of himself as food would have been. The stillness of endurance, the harsh identity of suffering, a self who seemed to have no ego. He couldn't complain to the forest or the water or the sky, the playground had no manager, no fun-maker paid to sell litter, nature has no wastes, not even me. More than new experience. It was a new way of experiencing. He could only accept. And ask. The low point was a high point. It would get lower.

The dawn was cloudy, overcast. The beginning of the seventh full day. He set out by following the water's edge, near five o'clock, drinking from time to time and looking for fish he knew he couldn't catch and plants he might risk eating. The narrow lake was really a big stream. It flowed slowly in two wide shallow channels separated intermittently by long ridges of rock and gravel. He found flowers and buds and young leaves, and tried green berries and had to spit them out. The stream went for miles, hours, and when it seemed like a promising route, around ten, it began to soak its way into marshes and bogs. He went as far as he could without walking in water over his boots. He heard splashes, made by frogs, he thought, but he saw none and waited and found none. He made his way back to where he could enter the forest and get to higher ground. But first he drank, from servings in cupped hands, taking a long time as if he were making a meal of water. The overcast had deepened. He decided to go without the sun, sloping upward and to his right, east and south.

Within yards, as he knew he would, he lost all direction. But the slope was evident, and slight, though for him it was hard going. The woods were passable, with heavy stands of evergreens that he could circle, fewer as he got higher, changing to birch and other trees, some like big bushes with what he thought were maple leaves. He took to resting at the birches and peeling bark away and scraping out the thin layer of inner pulp and eating it doggedly. He didn't get much for the work he put in, but it made him feel less helpless. Near midday the slope seemed to level off, and he had no way of knowing where to go. He decided to keep moving subjectively straight and gamble that he would tend to circle to his right. But in a long while, into the afternoon, he heard noises like a huge prolonged hiss and then he felt the rain.

It seemed light at first, despite the noise, but before long the trees began to drip, and he realized how hard it was raining. There was no shelter. The birches were too high and slender, the evergreens too low to the ground, and none of the other kinds were heavy enough. His hair was soaked, and his pants. The bush shirt was still dry inside, and his boots weren't leaking yet. He kept looking, and he couldn't hurry. In a half hour he found a large pine tree with dead bottom branches about level with his head. It was better than being out in the downpour, but it was still no shelter. He looked around carefully for what he might use, and set about gathering long pieces of deadwood and laying them aslant the bare branch stumps of the pine. When that was done he cut a supply of flat-leaved evergreen boughs, and shaking off the excess water, he placed them on top of the deadwood. When he was finished he had a crooked canopy some six feet long by four that looked like a teetering pile of rubbish suspended in mid-air. But it was relatively dry beneath it. He had to sit. He had spent his strength in making the shelter and his head ached strangely as if his whole skull were closing him in. Tension, he imagined, and hoped, and the memory of near disaster.

He decided to risk a fire. Below the edge of the canopy he cleared the ground of old brown pine needles until he was at bare earth. He poked at it with the unpointed end of the fishing stick and saved a small mound of earth in case he needed it to put out the fire. He got strips of birch bark, put some on the wet earth, tinder on that, more strips, and dead twigs from the pine tree, all small and unpeaked so that the flames wouldn't reach the canopy. It started easily and settled quickly. He watched it and kept it small. He enlarged it a little as the rain fell harder. It hissed and spit and made small explosions of sparks. And he decided that another small fire would be safer than one big one. The canopy leaked, a steady flow at the lower end, and water ran down the trunk of the pine. He went out and got dead branches to sit on, not breaking them in any way, for he had no strength to waste, and when things got worse he removed his boots, stuffed his two socks in one, removed his light shirt which was still fairly dry, and shoved that into the other boot. The boots he placed soles up between the thick branches he was sitting on. At least something would stay dry. He put the bush shirt back on and tried to adapt to the wetness and wait out the rain.

The forced idleness made him vulnerable. There were so many things wrong he had only to think of one to be overwhelmed by all of them. He watched the woods and tried not to think at all. The fires, as always, were distracting. They kept him busy and gave a low warmth to his feet and made him feel less miserable. The rain could go on all day. And all night. Another worry. You can't sleep in the rain, you'd lose body heat, and . . .

"So don't. Stay up and keep the fire going."

"It's not even three o'clock."

"This could be over in ten minutes."

"Sure."

He tried to remember the amount of food he'd had, the intake as compared to normal meals, home and abundance, restaurants, drinks that seemed so rich in retrospect, the caloric expenditure that had to come from his own body, the margins, the limits, a new and frightening clarity of mind, vision to see illusion by. It was futile. Somebody in some lab had probably figured it out, wrong. With no stress, or fear, or loss of heat, or pain, and desperate work. Would it help to know? A time when. Is it even possible to know it?

"Yeah, but then there's no need for it."

You don't measure life, living. It's just there. Or it isn't.

From out of himself then to looking at trees, for birches to cut into for their pulp, for some kind of resin on the evergreens and where it might be, on forks or leaves or buds, for plants that weren't there, moss and fungus. His awareness went freely inside, as new and directionless, it seemed, as when it went outside to the overpowering growth around him. Go deeply enough into it, and stay, and it reveals a meaning. Vision to see by. Presence. More than one.

A misshapen tree kept catching his eye. It was some forty feet away, not a birch, and it had a bulge on its trunk as if a limb had never grown. It was hard to make it out among the other trees. He didn't remember if he'd seen it before, or if it hadn't been there to be seen. The rain and the runoff gave it a sort of motion, but it didn't change position. As he watched it, it seemed more and more unusual, and he decided to trust his judgment.

He stripped to the waist, rolled the T-shirt into the heavy shirt and tucked the bundle with his boots. He took the fishing stick and set out quietly. The rain felt surprisingly warm and the ground was soft against his feet. As he got closer he saw that the bump was rounded, some ten feet up the trunk, like a mass of twigs but pointed, like thorns, and it twitched a little, and then he knew: a ball of quills, a porcupine, frightened, untouchable. How does it know?

"It can smell you."

"In the rain?"

"Why not? Your clothes stink. You scared it."

It didn't move. He could reach it with the fishing stick, but he decided against trying to impale it. It would only mean an unnecessary struggle. He looked around for a stout club and saw nothing that would do. The deadwood was brittle and slippery and partly rotted and the wrong shape. He finally picked a likely branch and began whittling at it with his penknife. It took time and he used it to plan what he'd do. And as he got closer to having a club, he felt himself getting more and more nervous. It wasn't just hunger and weakness anticipating relief, and it wasn't that if he missed he'd have no food. It was more than that. A meaning. Something to do with life. It would be easier if he were angry, if he imagined the thing as an enemy. Even fishing goes that way, with roars and yells, I got the bastard, and cheers, sport. Women don't seem to be good at it. It was different now. Need gave him another awareness, more basic than having an enemy.

He had the club. He tried dislodging the porcupine by levering it with the fishing stick, but it clung too tightly. Then with the fishing stick in his left hand he pushed the front quills back to expose its head and struck hard, once, with the club. The animal slipped clingingly and fell to the ground, still moving. And he clubbed it twice more.

It looked small with the quills down, no bigger than a cat, and shorter. He took it by one leg and brought it close to the shelter. The rain hadn't let up. He took the socks out of one boot and stuffed them into the other. He was shaking as he worked. The empty boot he placed under the runoff at the low end of the canopy and let it take water. With the penknife he cut the animal's head off and held it by the legs and let it bleed into the boot. When that was done, he forced himself to drink. A lot of it spilled down his neck and he washed it away with the rain. He rinsed the boot under the runoff.

It took a long time to skin the animal, carefully avoiding the quills, and to separate the offal from the meat. He recognized the liver, which seemed big for a small animal, and kept only that of the organ meats. He broke the carcass into manageable parts, rinsed them in the rain, and laid them out on boughs. The offal he put some distance from the shelter, and he washed himself over and over again in the trickling runoff from the canopy. He took off his pants and hung them by the belt from one of the crosspieces. He would chill less without them. Then he stoked the fires and made pointed sticks and crouching over the flames he began to roast some of the meat. The feeling of strangeness never left him. He was wet and naked and felt dirty with offal. A need was being met, and none of it was pleasurable, not even at last eating meat, which was tender.

He ate in bits and pieces, hungry for fat, barely cooking the chunks so that he could handle them. There was nothing culinary about it, it wasn't a meal all set out for the eating, it was a slow consuming of the dead animal, to last as long as something was left. The evening came early without the sun, and the fires made the forest look darker. Near seven the rain subsided a little and the canopy lost its runoff and began to drip less and less. He hung out his shorts and put on the dry socks and boots and went gathering a pile of small firewood. The work, light as it was, made him feel queasy. He put the heavy shirt over his shoulders and hunched near the flames. The woods would stay wet all night, perhaps for days, and he knew he wouldn't be able to lie down. It was going to be the longest night yet.

The queasiness remained. He stopped eating and cooked the rest of the meat thoroughly and sat still and waited. It subsided and returned and seemed to set up a cycle, growing worse. Somehow it didn't surprise him, from the very first his nervousness should have warned him. He held on as long as he could, and as the cycle tightened he moved away from the fires into the dark woods. And there with tremors and great heaves he vomited what seemed like everything he had eaten.

He was on all fours by the time it was over, and he crawled away unsteadily. It left him weak and almost broken. He tried to get to his feet and couldn't and he burst out weeping before he knew it. He didn't resist, he let his feelings run their course, the closest he'd been to panic. And relief.

When he was able to stand he wiped his hands and knees with the shirt and returned to the fires. He sat huddled, accepting the night, empty even of thought.

19

The rain ended around two in the morning and later the trees stopped dripping and the woods were quiet except for small animals wondering about the fires and the wastes he had made. He dressed as his clothes got dry enough and he dozed more deeply in the welcome silence. The birds started early and he watched all around him for the first signs of dawn, which would be north of east. It came gradually as a vast red background to his right. He let the fires go out. And in time between the trees an orange sun appeared that was soon too strong to look at. He remembered he was on an elevation. The woods looked more open, bigger. The camp was just a place that hadn't worked. It was full of bad memories, scattered leavings, a leaky shelter, sickness, and no sleep. The meat was gone. He wouldn't have wanted it anyway. The dampness would stay for days. It was 5:32. He walked away from it, going south.

He was weak, as he feared he would be, and hungry and aching, and jumpy from lack of sleep. The ground was too wet to sit on. And when he rested, standing, his legs began to tremble. It was better to stay on the move. He kept veering toward the sun, the easiest way, and realized he was looking for a clearing though he knew it was too early for anything to be dry. He tried to bring himself to decide on a course and stay with it, but he could summon no good reasons for it. His thoughts had become feelings. A time for mistakes.

"It's too far away."

South was losing its meaning. And his feelings were crossing limits he hadn't reached yet. Or maybe he had. Or would, soon.

"Maybe. You don't know."

It didn't seem worth arguing about.

"You have no choice."

The sun had even less meaning, except that he could see it. It guaranteed nothing. Only south.

"Make up your mind."

He kept going. He stayed on the heights wherever they went, largely southeast, for he remembered the swamps that might still be below him to his right. To rest he stopped at birches and dug out strips of inner bark. He made a routine of it, deliberately, and kept it regular and monotonous, speculating only about that, and when he had no birches he tried the tips of the evergreens until he found some that were palatable. The yield was scanty, but it was a game he could resent, and it gave a safe focus for his feelings.

The woods seemed endless. The high ground lev-

eled off and stayed flat for hours, which he tried to estimate as miles. In the underbrush his pants became
soaked from the knees down, chilly and dragging,
heavier than usual, and in time the sleeves of his bush
shirt were wet right through. He grew obstinate about
the routine, stopping, taking bearings, scraping food
where he could, advancing slowly. The continued
effort didn't lull him, it gathered fear like a momentum
as it went along. His fatigue generalized itself into a
physical despair. It made him less and less caring, not
yet reckless or hurried, but obsessed with the one idea
of finding a clearing to sleep in, and south. He had to
pass up trees that might have shown him the slope of
the land, and he knew he'd be too weak for any but the
smallest tasks. He couldn't prepare for alternatives. He
wondered what, if anything, he could have judged or
done differently.

It was early afternoon before things changed, and
they did before he was aware of it. He was into tall
brush, high tangled bushes like chokecherry trees, and
he realized there was a lot of light overhead and then
all around him. But no trees. The brush seemed im-
passable. He pushed on anyway, without choice, and
remembered how thickly things grew on the edge of
forests, and broke through into a rugged plain studded
with dead trees, broken and skeletal, looking like sil-
houettes against the horizon. The aftermath of a fire. It
went as far as he could see. The ground was covered
with new growth, spindly but obvious trees and plants
of all sorts, lush and green from being in the open. He
couldn't tell how long ago it happened. The bugs

emerged as he walked through the foliage. He ignored
them, as he had to. He was glad to be in the sun.

The last effort had been too much. He felt suddenly
weaker, drained of any strength or will. And for one
terrifying moment he was dizzy and faint, unable to do
anything but let himself crumble forward to the
ground careful not to impale himself on the fishing
stick. He fought to stay conscious, turned on his back
to undo his belt and remove the stick, and rolled again
to get on all fours, to kneel finally and look around for
a place to crawl to. To his right, south he noticed from
habit, some hundred feet away, was a dark hillock,
bare, razed by fire he thought, extending he knew not
how far, the only elevation in the plain. He managed to
get to his feet, dragging the stick safely behind him,
and stumbled his way forward, slipping to his knees
when he knew he was falling. It was an outcropping of
rock, more or less smooth, in ragged folds and steps
with mosses growing where they could. He reached it
on all fours and worked his way to the flattened top.

To his surprise he could see the country around him.
But he didn't stand up for a better view. His only intent was to stretch out. He pushed the stick to one side
and checked the time for no good reason, two-twenty-
something, and the sun which could burn him, and
eased himself face down on the rock. He felt the
warmth of it through his pants and shirt, and despite
the hard surface he let himself drift into unconscious-
ness without trying to get comfortable.

He kept waking cleanly and sleeping again, remembering no dreams and not imagining he was anywhere

else. He felt he knew the time and where the sun was, as if sleep were a journey, and he understood that what was going on in his head wasn't real, though some of it had to be true. He saw returns dwindling to nothing and certain kinds of limits that would be reached only once, hunger was a high barrier growing with the climbing, impossible, meant only for falling off into nowhere. An image of a vast distance persisted, placeless and vaster than anything he could ever know, and it stayed till he awakened and sat up. He really didn't know the time, he had to look at it, 6:09, the sun west, low, an hour and a half left. And with that the thought of home and the people who made it. The vast distances were all around him.

He got on one knee to look at the country, not daring to stand on the heights, and saw that it sloped downward for miles in all directions and rose in the distance, it seemed, to make a huge rim at the horizon. He studied it for a while, hoping to fix it in mind, for he would not see it again in the same light, and finally he slid down the rock and got to his feet a little unsteadily. He looked for plants, which he started tasting, and wood, not plentiful in this scrub, which he brought to the lee side of the outcropping. He found broadleaves and put them to use, glad to see that he wasn't sick intestinally. He pulled up enough weeds and grasses and plants to make something to sleep on, and he had to gouge out turf to make sure a fire wouldn't spread. The small tasks were long and heavy, the measure of his strength. And when they were done he kept roaming, the rock visible against the sky, and gathered wood

208

past sunset into deepening twilight. It was a tiring way of avoiding his thoughts.

The tinder in the sunglass case was still wet. He removed the case from his belt, the knotted handkerchief from his pocket, and sprinkled the contents into the hanky and put everything on a ledge of rock away from the breeze. Then he took out his wallet and brooded over the receipts, the licenses, the charge cards—the resources of another world. He decided on money, two fives and a ten which he could barely read, crumpled each bill, made a mound of twigs over them and set fire to the closest one. He added wood as needed and sat on the pile of weeds and leaned his back against the still warm rock. He thought nothing of the money, it had become more significant as paper. The receipts would be a record, probably never a souvenir. Of what? A motel, a gas station, a specific date? And for whom? The rest was an identity that had no existence, a coded fiction, it could only work with other fictions, enforced by law to seem real. 4501 160 001 693, it said on the card, S—p—e—n—c—e—r M—o—r—i—s—o—n.

"You."

"Me."

He left the fire and climbed part way up the rock and lay back once more. The whole sky was full of stars, the moon just past first quarter, north unmoving, more reliable than the sun, the Milky Way thickening in the south, an illusion, it had no south, just him looking at it from earth. There was too much to see. After a while he simply gazed at the entirety, without thoughts, or words, his feelings deep and quiet for the moment, and slowly he began to wonder about himself, unafraid still, and what would be the end of his efforts.

"You'll have to accept it."

He didn't have to ask what and he didn't try to deceive himself. There was no evading or denying anything, it could happen, was in fact happening, unless . . . He could see nothing but dreams and wishes.

On impulse he climbed down, took an armful of small firewood and twigs, brought it to the very top of the rock, and went back again for a flaming firebrand. He set fire to the pile with a sort of suppressed fury and urged it to blaze. It cast a lot of light around him, hiding the stars and defining the rock against the night. It would be seen for miles over the countryside and more in the sky. He felt like a primitive imploring the gods. But he knew there were no gods. He went back down.

From below it was impressive, a beacon that should be made to burn all night. But he had to let it be, he couldn't keep climbing to stoke it. He lay down on the weeds, aware of the glow of two fires, and stared at the night between them until an exhausted sleep made it all into nothing.

It seemed to last for a long time. What first entered his consciousness was that he hadn't stoked the fire. He wasn't chilly. In fact, it was warm. And then he was struggling mightily not to be wrong about something, but he saw it with a clarity beyond doubt: they were there as plain as the sunlight they stood in. Did you see the fire, is that it, is that it? Yes, right away, we were looking for it, you know, and we flew and flew. He couldn't see their faces because the sunlight was behind them. Gerry, is that you? A suspicion tried to belie his senses. Is Betty with you? They had stopped moving. Where's the plane? Their voices were pressures in the air, an environment of soundless words. How did you land here? Silence now, and judgment. Why is it daylight if . . .? Betty? Then it stopped, and he knew, and began forgetting.

The sun was up, full and strong, warming everything. He was facing east, almost straight into it. He rolled to his side and sat up slowly, heavy with a disappointment that eluded him, and in time he stood up painfully and climbed to the top of the rock. He noticed the ashes. A ritual, no more, performed in hope. It was still a good thing to have done. He examined the countryside as he awakened fully, and tried to decide where to go.

The south was sidelit by the early sun, miles of dense green made deeper by long shadows. The terrain dipped and rose as he'd seen yesterday, forming a strung-out lowland whose direction was hard to tell. He could see no clearings, no spaces glistening in the sun, only the black hollows that didn't reveal what they contained. It was all there was to see, and it gave him no choice. He got ready, gathered what plants he could, and set out once more, down the slow incline, not turning around, the rock already out of mind, past the line of burnt trees and into the still damp forest.

In a half hour he realized how weak he was. The long sleep had rested him somewhat and eased his mind a little, but it hadn't made him any stronger. He moved ahead slowly, at less than a stroll, taking time to find the easiest passages and keeping his meanders on a rough course. It was movement with the sun, its light and shadows always changing, every bearing wrong. He could have no destination, no arriving, could expect nothing but what appeared in front of him, and he had nothing to tell him how many miles he'd traveled and what they meant on a straight line south. The woods had become familiar, a varying sameness of experience, and he recognized trees he knew but couldn't name. In time he'd have to call them something. It was primal, and pointless. But he knew them, had come to know them over time, and that seemed to be reason enough. A human act, to give names to things: the tree with the wrapped-around bark. He even stopped and touched it. It wasn't pointless any more, it was too primal. He had confirmed something and he wondered what. The tree with several trunks. So little time. And then he thought of the cigarettes.

"You lost count."

There were sixteen in the warped package. He had to count them three times to be sure. He couldn't remember when he'd thrown out the last one. And worse, he wasn't sure how many he'd started with. Something around twenty. It was more than a puzzle in arithmetic. He feared for his memory. It was important, crucial, to know the number of days. Days left.

"No!"

One has no bearing on the other.

"Forget it. It'll come back to you."

The days won't come back.

"No. They won't."

"Then it doesn't matter."

"Yeah."

There was no future to calculate, only the sun making the day and what he could find in its light. Even less. It was what he could stumble across, something already there that he might miss. He couldn't know, and it was futile to try to know. Clock and calendar were fantasies compared to his awareness, day was the moving light of day, and darkness was the world standing in its own shadow. A turn would change it. A turn of self. The tree with the ribbed leaves. He touched that too, and wondered what was happening to his mind.

He saw no animal tracks, found no clearings, no water. He was two days without it now. He rested longer when he found dry places. Twice he heard and then saw large birds flutter away clumsily as he approached, some sort of partridge. By their sounds they didn't seem to go far, but he didn't have the strength to pursue them. Well past midday when the ground lost its downward slope and stayed level, he expected to see gaps or thickets and an end to the woods. But the forest didn't change. And in late afternoon the terrain began to rise again. He followed it doggedly until he felt he was on high ground. And he knew he should go no farther.

He took a long time to make camp, collecting twigs and wood, and making a place for a fire. He couldn't break off even the smallest evergreen boughs. He cut them one by one, needles not flat leaves this time, and finally had a pile thick enough to insulate him from the damp ground. He was too tired to notice that he was dizzy. He used the last of the tinder. And he couldn't help being aware that he found the lighter hard to work. He lay down as soon as he could. It was easy to know what was needed, a place with food, a few days, and on to another one. Easy merely to decide, and useless.

"It doesn't depend on you."

"What does?"

Nothing. Or no answer. And a vast difference between them. He saw stars in patches of sky and heard life in the dark woods. The tree with the little white flowers. He'd have to look for it. The sun would come back and he knew he'd be traveling again, just to look for something to find. Not nothing. And not no answer.

Sounds woke him in the night and he crawled to the fire to stoke it. In a deep silence later, for he couldn't see the flames or hear their crackling, he became aware of a buzzing in his head. It was a low rushing pressure that gave the illusion of a distant rustle like leaves tossing in the wind. But there was no wind, and no rain, and leaves would be louder and close by. For a while he lay still, wondering if he was going to be sick, and when he moved, the noise of the boughs and his clothing covered up the buzzing. He sat up and let his own noises settle. The buzzing returned. Silently he put his hands over his ears. There was nothing. He took his hands away: noise. It was real, out there.

He stood up in the dark, returned to silence, and cupped his hands behind his ears and began a slow

214

turn to each side. The rustling increased in one direction and he scanned it again to make sure. Insects maybe, wasps, or bees, but he didn't think they'd be out at night. He used the open wallet to mark the direction, stoked the embers back to flame, found the fishing stick and used that as a better marker. The fire dispelled the distant sounds and he lay down again, to sleep.

The pre-dawn birds drowned out all but his personal noises. They chattered and shrieked and sang, all because of breakfast, and when he stirred they objected to his presence. As he waited for better light he searched for evergreen tips and resin and birches and ate whatever he could find. His fatigue was deep, as restrictive as an illness, which it was in a way, but less acute for the moment. Sounds made him feel his aloneness, he was the only one to hear them, and yet they drew him out of himself by their clarity. Vision wasn't contact, hearing was. Something else to think about. He couldn't hear any distant rustlings.

When the light was stronger, the sun flaring in pinpoints behind the trees, he took a reading along the fishing stick, a little west of south, and started walking again, carrying the stick and not looking at his watch for the time. The birds faded behind him and new ones scolded him as he passed. He became conscious of the noise his boots made in the undergrowth, the rustle of his clothing as he moved, twigs breaking and scratching, of his breathing, and at the least effort the thuds of his heartbeat. It all stopped when he did, and then he listened. The birds grew less insistent, having eaten by now, and chirped only intermittently. And even without distinct noises there seemed to be an atmosphere of sound, as if the sun had made things audible. Probably bugs and moving things and trees responding. But no noise like last night's.

The heights began to slope away from him, gently in front, south, and more and more sharply to his right. He decided to deviate downhill, west, 90° off course, hoping not to have to climb back up. The slope made the going easier for a while and then harder as he had to hold himself back. The ground got precipitous, rocky, full of thickets, the trees more rugged. He was in some sort of ravine, a mistake. And when he stopped to figure out what he'd have to do, and his noises stopped with him, he heard over his breathing the unmistakable rush of water. He kept going, slowly, the sounds increasing above his own noises, and was soon at the edge of a gorge, the rush now deafening, looking at the churnings of falls and rapids below him. Contact. Sounds beyond hearing. He trembled with elation, and a sort of fright.

"I—found—you!"

He couldn't hear his own words.

And he couldn't drink, yet.

The water started as a stream from above and dropped by steps over rocks and into shallows, gathering momentum at every fall, gushed through the channel below him, and fell again and again until finally it pooled some hundred yards away and perhaps forty feet down. It made noise and spray and its own rainbows. He held on to a tree and looked at it all with fas-

216

cination and worry. The thunderous hiss made hearing useless, and seeing wasn't enough, it could give no warning of danger, of loose wood, or different ground, and it even made close distances harder to perceive.

He climbed downhill, going from tree to tree, following the slope of the gorge and guiding himself by its tumult. Near bottom the rush subsided and he could hear the differing kinds of waters bubbling and trickling and changing into the easy flow of another stream. He came out of the woods onto a narrow gravel shore, crowded with bushes and thickets, and pushed his way past these to find a wide sunlit beach before him and water that went on and on and was wide enough to be a river. He squatted in a few inches of it and drank from his hands, glancing instinctively for fish.

It was past nine, and already hot. There were a few small white clouds, a breeze from the water, no signs of weather. He put on the capped handkerchief, took off the heavy shirt, things he had done before that seemed like rehearsals for this moment. But it was all different. He had fewer resources now, and hope only of his own making, a fantasy. Travel would be easier for a while, and he had water, with no way of carrying it, and he knew he couldn't take to the bush again without supplies of some kind. He walked in the new spaces, and stillness, and drank small amounts from time to time, and found nothing he could eat. He realized how arduous the woods had been, and listened with dread to the slow crunching of his boots. A diminished self.

The river relieved him of decisions. He had only to keep walking. The beach gave him an unobstructed route and no choice in direction. He could follow it without watching, or listening or taking bearings, which he did anyway to verify where it was going. It brought him more and more southwest. The opposite shore, some hundred feet over at first, got farther and farther away and became the far side of a lake, fed no doubt by other streams, two or three miles across. And by noon, with the heat as tiring as the bush, he was tending almost west, a course that would circle the lake, he estimated, and meet the distant shore. It would mean the bush once more, or marshes, or some new thing he couldn't anticipate. Wasted miles, and far off course, but easier for now. He could only know by walking.

The scrub to his left became forest again, thinly wooded here and there, and in these places he rested and made note of them as possible routes in case he should have to return. The distant shore seemed to get nearer. It took hours before he could see it with any perspective and actually notice that he was approaching it. Gradually he was able to make out that it had been running at a diagonal away from him. As he got closer and closer he saw the wide gap of a bay ahead and followed the turning shore, left, the sun passing in front of him, and advanced, watching the waters, until he realized that the shores weren't going to meet. The lake was still a river, and it was going south.

He was too tired to make camp. He drank a little and didn't wash. The sun was getting lower, not yet red.

There were a few clouds. He scraped away the stones from a section of beach and simply lay down, trying to remember the unmarked days, glad at not having to move any more, and gave in to his exhaustion.

It was early morning twilight when he awoke, things still gray, a little after three, the river shining without detail. He got up painfully and slowly, became aware of the ever-present birds. He had been thinking of ways to fish, and none seemed practical. He wound his watch and shivered and began walking to get warm. He stumbled at first but kept it up. Only the river made a difference. He let it decide and followed it obsessively.

He saw the dawn break over the forest and felt the warmth of the sun as it got higher and finally its heat as it rose into full morning. Close to nine the time on his watch surprised him. He knew it was right, but it didn't correspond with the feelings he had about his movements. He was sure he had stopped to rest from time to time, but he couldn't remember doing it. He knew he hadn't eaten. And that it was hot. He didn't stop. Around ten-thirty the river made a long turn to the southeast and snaked back and forth and held to its new course. There were clearings at the turns and he picked small plants at random and ate them as he found them. The direction worried him a little, and the heat. And he decided to wait out the hours around noon. He remembered making that decision, and then nothing.

He came to himself in the bush, face-down. He was in his T-shirt, lying in matted leaves and pine needles, a few feet from the trees around him. He got on all fours and managed to sit up, dizzily. The hanky was on his head, but the stick was gone, and his shirts. He could see brightness and clearing to his right—the river, he concluded, and wondered if he might be wrong. It was after five. Since noon. Terror seized him for a moment and made his heart beat fast. He waited, and it passed.

"It's started."

There was nothing to know, nothing to judge. It would happen by itself.

"Yeah. Oh, yeah."

"That was the risk."

He tried standing, and made it. He went toward the brightness, noticing the tracks he'd made, and saw the beach and the river. His head was clear enough, he knew the directions, what he'd been doing. Without having to consider, he retraced his steps and found the light shirt, the heavy one, and farther away the stick. He knew why he'd dropped it first.

There was something wrong with the sun. It wasn't where it should be. He lined up the watch and knew before he made the calculation that the river was now running east. He hadn't been in the bush all those hours, he had been walking. And he'd never know how long. East. He checked it again. There was no mistake about it. And nothing to be done.

He decided against making camp. He knew it was unwise not to stop early, but camp meant sitting and worrying over things and being afraid. There were two hours of sun left, and another two of light, and it wasn't hot any more. He drank and splashed water on his face and didn't feel any better. He had to see where the river was going.

He walked unsteadily into the evening, and followed his lengthening shadow until it disappeared, and he continued into the twilight. The river went northeast for a while and straightened, still east, and widened, it seemed, and offered no crossings. He could see its presence in the incomplete darkness and hear it moving gently at his side. The dipper showed him Polaris, and Polaris gave him north, accurate beyond doubt. There was no mistake. The certitudes were tangible. Fully dressed he scuffed out a place to lie in, and did so, more than aware of slipping into this kind of sleep. Tomorrow did not have to exist. He was less afraid than he had feared.

The river stayed on his mind all night. It wasn't a worry, or a hope. It was more basic, a confirmation that he was still there, able to know, a sort of contact with the next day. He awoke before light, feeling worse, and had to crawl to the water's edge to revive himself. He remembered the watch, and wound it where he was, on all fours, twisting with the pains in his stomach. He struggled to his feet and stayed up and began to walk, swaying, dragging the stick behind him, and kept close to the bush, looking for food as the light got stronger. He rested at bends in the river. They never went south for long, they returned east and northeast.

He continued into the morning, into the growing heat, and as the sun got higher, he took to watching for a place in the bush, with luck near a clearing, where he

221

could spend the hot hours. But some time after ten, the river began to widen. And little by little he could see that it was forking around a point of land. It didn't look like another bay. In a half hour he was abreast of it, a few hundred yards over, an island most likely, and saw that his own shore up ahead was going to turn to his right, southeast. He simply forgot about his plans and kept going, not stopping to rest. The point became the far shore and continued indefinitely, too far to tell if it was an island. He entered the southeast turn, anxious to see where it led.

He couldn't see the end of it. Miles of water, on course, lost to sight in the distance, disappearing into the forests on the horizon. All blazing in the noon sun. He began coming across things he hadn't noticed seeing, a big rock to avoid, a fallen tree, the beach narrow enough to make him wade. And then he found himself looking at terrain that was suddenly new and that he couldn't remember approaching. His watch told him only the current time, past twelve, and he couldn't connect it with anything. It was like yesterday, he realized, a loss of continuity, blackouts. And the same terror, which passed. But there was the river, and he was still on his feet. A few more miles and he'd know. He'd know what? He couldn't answer, or argue. He tried to force himself back to his mind, to judge. He wasn't traveling in the bush, he couldn't get lost, or wander, he had a shore he could follow, no matter how. There was nothing to decide.

He wet the hanky for coolness. And when he tried to do something about the things he was carrying, the two shirts and the fishing stick, he became puzzled and disoriented, a new problem. It absorbed him completely and took on immense importance. Without debate or thought, he simply went into the bush and sat down to work on it. Or so it seemed. He eased down to one side, unconscious, and kept coming to, understanding more and more of what was happening, and let himself sleep. The river was still there.

It was past three when he was able to stay awake, a little more clearheaded, and to do things with conscious intent. He went to the water and drank and looked at the running river. Working clumsily he secured the heavy shirt to the back of his belt, not to lose it. The other shirt he finally made into a crude rope by rolling it along the extended sleeves. He tied both cuffs to the stick just under the fork, and draped the ensuing sling over one shoulder and across his chest. He wet the hanky again and started trudging along the shore. He'd know.

The terrain revealed itself so slowly that changes seemed sudden. In the distance the river appeared to be widening, and in time the other shore began to stand out against a yet farther shore. And then clearly it had water behind it: an island. Past it the two streams met and made the river look twice its size. It held to the southeast. For a long time. Close to an hour. And he began to think it might be permanent. Gradually he saw more and more water in the distance, a horizon of bush miles away, the other shore turning and disappearing to the south. The river was emptying into a huge lake.

He knew his own shore would turn. He expected it to go east again and circle the lake. Tomorrow's work. He saw more and more of the vast stretch of water. And the beach turned, left, and he saw yet more water, and it kept turning, and he saw no shore that was going to circle the lake. It wasn't a lake. It was another river. It came from the north and went south. And he couldn't cross it. He now knew.

20

The sun was warming him, he began to realize, and it was day. He felt stones hurting the side of his face. His arms itched and then ached sharply as if they were full of needles. And as he stirred with that, the rest of his pain jarred him awake and he remembered his despair at seeing the other river. His throat felt swollen with thirst. The heavy shirt was over his head and along his back. It struck him as odd, why not wear it. He pulled it from him, not entirely, and saw the bright beach. In stages he levered himself to one haunch and finally sat up. He was in his T-shirt, which was torn and dirty. His arms were badly bitten, and red, and sore from burning. They didn't look like his own, but the watch was his. The rivers gleamed in the morning sun.

He saw the light shirt close by, still on the fishing stick, with one cuff untied. He must have given up on it. The knotted hanky was next to it. He thought nothing of it, but something felt strange. He noticed scuff marks in the gravel, and tracks, dragged out and irregular, leading to the bush and from it. It seemed like a long way, forty, fifty feet. And all around him. His pants were torn, and his knees were scraped and had been bleeding. There were more tracks to one side, and small branches of deadwood next to them. He'd been working, to no avail. He remembered none of it.

"Not—at—night." It was an inarticulate whisper.

And not on arriving. He'd been exhausted, he must have slept where he'd stopped.

"And not this morning."

He looked at the time: four-twenty-something. The sun was too far up for that, it was eight, or nine. The second hand wasn't moving, and when he listened to it, the watch wasn't ticking. A whole day had gone by, and two nights. Maybe more, but at least a day. He couldn't bring himself to believe it.

He checked everything again: the tracks, the shirts, his reasoning such as it was. He slipped the watch from his wrist and tapped it. It didn't start. He wound it the way he always did, though more shakily. It took a lot of winding: it hadn't just stopped, it had really run down. The fact was there, and its meaning. And the fear that went with it. It was more than blackouts now.

He wouldn't be going anywhere, not back to the falls to cross, and not north along the river. He knelt in the gravel and started laying out his things, coins, keys, wallet, the cigarettes, the ball-point. He kept the penknife. He did it all neatly, to keep a discipline of sorts. Somehow that seemed important. He became aware of his body as weakness, and pain, which could only get worse. His arms were thin where they weren't swollen with bites, muscles and tendons visible under the skin. The comb, the short bottle opener, the lighter. He put the lighter back in his pocket. His belt was too long. He hadn't been that size since he was twenty. The years weren't years. This would be the place. Where the two rivers meet. And then the time. His mind felt clear with absurdities.

"It's not going to be . . . quick."

"And not while you're up."

It seemed to make sense. He brought himself to one knee and tried to crouch and from there to stand. But his legs wouldn't support him. He crawled to the water's edge and drank and doused his head repeatedly. Then he tried again to stand and fell over into the water, and tried again and again until he was on his feet and shuffling precariously toward the bush.

There he leaned on trees and crept on the soft ground and gathered small branches into a scattered pile. It took a long time. Bugs collected in clouds around him. And in another long while he hooked the twigs crudely into the forks of a longer branch, and he dragged the whole thing to the beach, crawling, and standing, and letting himself down before he fell. He broke some into kindling by kneeling on them and stacked the rest for a fire. They wouldn't last very long. He went back and got more, and put on the light shirt as a help against the bugs and went back again. There was no thinking to it, or planning, or even deciding. As long as he was conscious, he was making camp. The alternative was to wait, and know, and that was worse. Or so he thought.

He was still on his feet when it started. He was stumbling toward the bush to escape the sun and to look for whatever he could eat. And in what seemed like the next moment he was on all fours, still moving, not yet in the woods, and conscious enough to know that he was passing out in mid-movement. The coolness told him he had got there. And in a while he knew the bugs were plaguing him. And then he knew he was returning to the beach, his knees bleeding again, and that he was covering his head with the heavy shirt, something he'd done before. The phases were like seizures of sudden sleep, he knew of them when they were over. He wondered how long it would be this time. It was waiting of a different kind.

The question was on his mind when he came to. It was late afternoon. The sun was softer, and pleasant, the kind of light you get after work, just before supper. There's sports news on the radio and the last traffic reports. Noise outside from the kids, when they're young, and TV. You can always tell when it's on. Small things, like the color of the plates. Living.

"Betty . . ."

The clarity of being home, as acute as his pain.

"It doesn't look . . ."

His watch was running: it was the same day. Without it he'd never know. The sun was useless now, only the moon could count the days. He looked for planes, in case, and didn't feel absurd. That had been the purpose, to get closer. He wondered how far he'd come, how long they'd looked. Weeks now. It must be over. It was futile to calculate. What time remained was inside, was himself, spilling out. He felt a new fear gathering

228

around him and he crawled away from it as though it were a presence. He forced himself to think of what he could rig to catch fish, and he tried to get up to be doing something, but it all faded again. And it became sunset. The same day.

"The pen might do."

He began working on the ball-point. He was much weaker. His fingers shook at the slightest effort. He had to make sure he was twisting it the right way and had to use his teeth and two hands to loosen it. The threading fascinated him, it seemed so out of place here. He took the pen apart and removed the cartridge, careful not to lose the spring, and started scraping the tip on a flat stone. He could barely hold on. When the point was ragged and scratchy, he tried to bend the cartridge in his fingers, but he wasn't strong enough. He tried it under his boot, an awkward position, and the gravel kept giving way, on the stone, and he couldn't press hard enough. He had to stop.

He thought about it and pictured what he'd need, a point of support, something to grip with, and finally he slipped the cartridge into an eye at the base of his boot and slowly pulled on it with both hands. It bent and folded. He did it again, badly, with the top end. Then he pressed the two ends across each other in a crude X. The point he left sticking up a little, the blunt end he pressed as flat as he could. He had a hook of sorts. He could hardly move his arms.

It was late twilight. He untied his boots and pulled at the laces, hole by hole, a slow task, for they were long, and when they were free he tied them into one length. It gave him some ten feet of line. He tied one end to the twisted cartridge, the point facing the line, and made a loop around the X to give it support. The other end he fastened to the fishing stick just above the forks. And the rig was ready.

It had taken all his strength to do it. He sat cross-legged and hunched over, unwilling to lie down until it was all done, and wondered what to use for bait. He watched the darkness settle and felt the coolness from the river. The stars were visible, unclouded, a rising moon a few days from full, the sky waiting for tomorrow's sun. It would have to be tonight, no matter what the effort.

He fumbled three bills from the wallet and used them to start the fire, twenties he saw when he lit them. He kept the blaze small to save wood and sat next to it to feed it. The light would attract insects, moths, big ones, and he'd have bait. He'd plant the stick in the river at knee depth and the rig would do the rest. He waited, and planned, and even hoped.

But he had already spent himself. He felt a slight dizziness, then the momentary seizure of sleep, and more, and tried to fight it off and couldn't. He'd have to set up the rig next time he came to. He managed to move away from the fire and he crawled more and more into nothingness.

He didn't do it the next time. He couldn't even get to his knees. He was aware of day, and heat, and of deciding things that drifted into vague dreams, memories he couldn't be sure of. There was a nighttime, and a fire, and presences, and no words to know them by. Once, it was raining a little. He kept slipping in and out of consciousness. He knew he'd taken his boots off. The waking told him he was still alive. The other kept arriving like nothing. At any moment it would stay.

"I—won't—know."

But somewhere within himself he thought he did.

21

They were standing over him, not saying anything. Three of them. There were others a little way off, and somebody at a fire doing something. No one spoke. The tall gaunt man in faded khakis was next to Spence, looking at him, just waiting. He was older than the others, in his fifties, with short graying hair and pale brown eyes as calm as his silence. His seriousness looked feigned, as though he could laugh at any moment. It was morning, early, around eight, and sunny, the sky full of white clouds. He adjusted slowly, daring to believe. It was lasting too long to be a dream.

Spence said, "You're really here."

The older man nodded casually. The others said nothing.

"Do you hurt?" the man asked, and waved a hand at Spence's legs. His voice was soft, resonant with overtones. It was good to hear it.

"No, nothing broken."

Involuntarily he put his hand to his stomach. The burns on his arms were obvious, and the bites. No need to explain. It was inside. He smelled insect repellent. His beard was wet, they had probably tried to make him drink. He was lying on evergreen boughs, not of his own making surely, and there was a cushion under his head. He was barefoot. They had bandaged his knees. He fingered the boughs.

"What are these?"

"Spruce," said one of the other men. He had probably done the gathering. They were younger, in their twenties, long black hair well groomed, in bright sport shirts. No one seemed to be in a hurry. He tried to sit up and they helped him. To his surprise he wasn't dizzy, just weak.

The other three were in their teens. One was cooking something in a pot over a small fire, the other two were trying to undo the laces that had become the fishing line. They were all watching him.

"Was that in the water?"

"Yes," said the other young man.

There was a short stick tied to the line as a float.

"Did you do that?"

"No."

"Did I?"

"I don't know."

"I must have."

The young man nodded once.

Two long aluminum boats were moored on the beach, their outboard motors tilted out of the water.

"Were you looking for me?"

"No," said the older man.

"How did you find me?"

"We saw smoke."

"Today? This morning?"

He nodded.

"I don't remember making a fire."

The man laughed. His whole face changed with the humor he was seeing.

"You burned your socks," he said.

Spence thought about it awhile and began to giggle and they all laughed with him as though an immense joke had worked. When you can't walk you burn your socks.

"What day is it?"

"Tuesday," said one of the young men.

"The date."

"The fifteenth."

"July, of course."

"Yes."

A long silence followed which wasn't embarrassing. They weren't asking him any questions. He thought of telling the teenagers to simply cut the laces and he'd tie them around the boots. But somehow he knew that wouldn't do, it would be wasteful, and he respected their work. He delighted in their vigor. And their presences.

He turned to the older man.

"My name is Morison. Spence Morison."

"John Sweetree."

He didn't introduce the others.

"I crashed, in a Cessna, over two weeks ago. Far from here, north, past the falls, the second lake past the falls. I lost the plane in the water. I was way off course. They couldn't find me. So I started walking south."

"With—this." He indicated Spence's things.

Spence struggled out the penknife and the lighter. "And this."

Sweetree grinned.

"It wasn't just socks. I burned money too."

They all laughed with him at that.

The teenager dipped a tin mug in what he was brewing, added water to it from the river, and brought it to Spence. It was broth from a fish soup, seasoned with herbs of some kind. He didn't ask which. While he drank it slowly, the two others threaded the laces to his boots and put them next to him. One of the young men gathered Spence's things in the bush shirt, tied it off and put it in one of the boats. Sweetree was at the boat, arranging something.

One of the teenagers came and sat next to Spence and said nothing for a long while. Finally he spoke.

"Mr. Morison, did you live in the bush before?"

"No, not really. It was my first time."

Nothing more was said. Spence put the boots on and tied the laces around them. It all but exhausted him. When it was apparent that he couldn't stand, the young men helped him to the shore and into one of the boats. He sat on the bottom near the stern, facing front, his back on a cushion against the seat. They shoved off a little and got in, Sweetree at the motor, a young man in the middle facing Spence, and a teenager at the bow. As the motor caught, Spence waved his thanks to the other three on the shore. They waved back, smiling, and the youngest said something in another language and they all laughed. Spence turned to look at Swee-tree.

"Nothing. Just Indian talk." He was still smiling.

He backed the boat and turned and let it gather its own momentum.

"Can you get to a radio? A sending radio?"

"I know. Yes."

"How long will it take?"

"The time it takes to go down the river."

"How long is that?"

"When it flows fast, a few hours."

The motor drowned out any talk that wasn't shouting. Spence watched the water. It was going south, and he was on it, with men who knew the country. To them it wasn't wilderness, nor in a way to him. He didn't try to anticipate events, they would happen. Time was his. The young man handed him a hat, an old-fashioned wide-brimmed affair, stained with use, the band long since gone, and from a thermos another cupful of broth. Spence saluted his thanks and sipped at it. The woods unfolded along the shores, dense and awesome, part of his knowledge now, different. The speed of the boat disturbed him for no reason he could find. Perhaps it was the motor, it seemed so powerful, inhuman. Perhaps the country had to be felt by foot, and hand. Or maybe he was just too exhausted to adjust. Maybe. July 15. He tried to count back over the days. Did June have thirty or thirty-one? The calendar seemed as artificial as the motor, and as real. He'd been gone nineteen or twenty days. Something had changed.

Around noon, sun time, the river entered another long lake, and near the far end he could see houses. They stayed far and small over the water and then suddenly they had size and detail, wooden houses, a few with screened porches, one larger than the others, some like shacks, three large gas tanks on scaffolded platforms. About a dozen people came out to see, women, children, mainly men. Sweetree eased the boat to a long wooden pier. The teenager jumped out and moored it and began talking to the onlookers in the other language.

Two men helped Spence out of the boat and led him up steps to a screened porch and sat him in a rocking chair. He almost laughed at the experience, he was sitting in a chair, a rocking chair at that, simple, intricate. Sweetree stayed at the pier and talked. There was no hurry.

A man with authority all over his face came out of the building and looked at Spence and frowned and took in the people at the pier. Late thirties, filled out, modern hair style, shaggy moustache, a little bald, dressed in the clichés of the engineer, work shirt with pleated pockets, clean pants, soft boots, he was almost stylish. Spence was torn and dirty, hair matted, debris in his beard. Only his watch looked like anything, large, expensive. The man saw it. The teenager came through the screen door with Spence's things and put them down on the floor.

"What's going on?" the man said. He had a slight French accent.

The teenager gestured to John Sweetree and left.

The man looked at Spence again and was about to say something and didn't. Spence said nothing. The situation would sort itself out.

The man turned to the house door, also screened, and said, "Stanley," in a deferential tone that tried to be pàlly. Noise from inside and another man came out, presumably Stanley. He was also in his thirties, lots of hair, the moustache, plain sport shirt, tailored work pants. He had a pipe. He looked at Spence, said, "Oh," and looked at the other man.

"They're new people," said the first man.

"So it appears," said Stanley. He seemed to have a different kind of authority. He turned to Spence, saw the watch.

"You're not a Cree, are you?" he said.

Spence looked at the man and waited before speaking.

"Right now, I don't know."

"Oh."

John Sweetree and the young man and the teenager were coming to the porch. No one spoke as they entered and stood about. Sweetree looked at Spence as if to check if everything was all right. His eyes seemed to say a great deal.

"How do you do," said Stanley to no one in particular.

"We found him in the bush."

"Indeed." He turned to Spence. "Were you lost?"

"My plane crashed."

"You're a pilot?"

"I'm licensed."

"Did you have any passengers?"

"Just cargo."

"Oh, uh, what company do you fly for?"

"None. I was on vacation."

"Oh. Oh! When did you crash?"

"About three weeks ago."

"Good heavens! Has anyone been looking for you?"

"I presume as much."

"I should imagine. Where are you from?"

"Montreal."

"We'll be glad to reach someone for you. Whom can we contact?"

"Henri Tétrault, at Chibougamau, he'd be listed."

"Yes, yes. And, uh, may I have your name?"

"Spencer Morison."

"And, uh, this Henri Tétrault will know of you, of course?"

"Yeah, he will."

"Splendid. We'll get on it immediately."

The two men went inside. Spence turned to Sweetree.

"Can we go down there?"

The two men helped him down the steps and a little distance from the porch. The teenager brought the chair for Spence and gave him more of the broth.

"Who are those people?" said Spence.

"The guy with the pipe, he's an anthro."

"What's that?"

"An anthropologist."

"Doing what?"

"He's studying Indians. Concepts of community land tenure. He'll get it all wrong."

"And the other man?"

"They don't know for sure. He's government in some way. Grants and contracts, there's lots of money around."

After a silence Spence said: "They didn't seem to be glad to see us."

"We weren't looking for work. When four men turn up, it looks like a demonstration."

"Are you from around here?"

Sweetree laughed.

"Yes and no," he said. "But I know what you mean. Farther north about a hundred miles past Mistassini."

"What brought you—you know, where I was?"

"I was showing the young people."

"Showing them what?"

"How we lived. Our way of life. They'll forget."

More silence, for a long time.

The two official men came down from the porch. They went directly to Spence and seemed a little more animated.

"Well, Mr. Morison," said the government man, "you've been very hard to find, it seems. Do you know, they were still searching when I called. How do you feel?"

"Fine. You got through all right?"

"Why, yes. Yes. They'll be sending a helicopter. Té-trault is informing Montreal. Allow me to introduce myself. I'm Dr. Jacques Desautels, supervisor of field

240

research, and this is Dr. Stanley Falconbridge, professor of anthropology."

"How do you do. This is Mr. John Sweetree, and two of his friends."

They nodded, and that was that.

"Can I get you a drink?" said Stanley. "Perhaps it would brace you up a bit."

"No thanks, this is fine." He held up the broth.

"If you'd care to clean up," said Desautels, "a change of clothes, we'd be only too pleased . . ."

"Thank you, I'll wait till I get to Henri's."

"I should imagine you're still a little under the weather from your experience." This from Stanley.

"Yes, I am."

"Well," said Desautels, "if there's anything you want, just give us a holler, we'll be inside."

"Thanks."

They left. Spence returned to his thoughts. And the wait began, broken by snatches of conversation whenever anybody wanted to talk.

It took hours for the plane, not a helicopter, to arrive. It was a four-seater with floats, and seemed to have more than one person aboard. Many hands moored it to the long pier. The two official men went to meet it. The pilot didn't get out, but two men in sport shirts did. One was carrying a camera around his neck, the other what looked like recording equipment. They looked over at the rocking chair.

"Mr. Sweetree," said Spence, "it's going to get busy. I want to thank you for everything."

"That's all right, it could've been anybody."

"Maybe. But it was you. I owe you my life."

"O—o—oh," he said doubtfully, "doesn't everybody owe somebody that?"

Spence had to think it over. And he laughed. They helped him toward the plane, the teenager bringing Spence's things. The man with the camera was taking pictures rapidly, the other held up a small microphone.

"How do you feel, Mr. Morison?"

"Like going home."

"What was it like out there?"

"Can't this wait?"

"You've been news, close to a month. And here it is the moment of rescue."

"How come you're here?"

"We were doing a follow-up on bush flying, safety, that bit, and we heard they found you."

"Yeah."

He finally got into the front seat, said "Hi" to the pilot, clasped John Sweetree by the shoulder, and watched him leave to stand with his friends. The reporters scrambled on. Soon they were taxiing and turning and into the takeoff, waving to the people on the pier. Too much was happening too fast. The noise of the plane discouraged any conversation. At least that.

The flying didn't bother him. He looked at the country below and kept looking. It was hard to believe that only this morning he was down there. He asked the pilot for his map and had him point out where they were. He studied it for most of the flight.

They landed at Henri's. There was a crowd on the

docks and up the road to the garages. Henri was the first one there, helping him get out of the plane.

"Mr. Morison, how are you? How are you?" He was excited.

"I'm okay."

"We looked and looked. Everywhere."

"I was way off course. I'm sorry . . ." The microphone intruded.

"No, no, no, no. You're alive!"

Gus was there, grinning, not butting in. Henri took charge quickly and got Spence in an old car and signaled Gus to get in. They eased past the crowd and drove off. Spence noticed that his station wagon was still there. In a few blocks and a few turns they arrived at a clinic where a young doctor was waiting.

He soon had Spence on an examining table, stripped to his drawers. Henri and Gus stood around, still grinning. The doctor spoke as he worked.

"Are you dizzy?"

"Not any more."

"Did you have water?"

"Most of the time, yes."

"What kind of food?"

Spence had to think about it.

"Leaves, you know, plants."

"Do you know what kind?"

"No."

"And today?"

"They . . . the people who found me . . ." It didn't sound right. "My friends gave me some soup."

"Oh, did you know them?"

"I do now."

"How much soup, what kind?"

"It tasted like a fish broth of some kind, with herbs, about four or five cups of it."

"In what period of time?"

"All day, till the plane came."

"No nausea?"

"No."

"Any cramps here?" He touched his stomach. "Pain?"

"No cramps. Less and less pain."

"How much do you normally weigh?"

"175, 180."

"You might've lost thirty pounds."

The doctor set up an intravenous apparatus.

"What's that for?"

"Glucose."

"In the vein?"

"Yes, of course."

"I don't want it."

"You're going to get it anyway."

"I don't want it. Soup will do, and whatever else I can keep down. And I'll take it this way." He indicated his mouth.

"But why? It's easier . . ."

"Because right now there's too much . . . No offense, doctor, there's just too much."

"All right. I think I know what you mean. You'll have to rest."

"I don't feel like doing anything else."

Gus and Henri helped him with his clothes.

"I'll get you some new stuff," said Henri. "You can stay at my house."

"That'd be great, Henri. I'd like to phone Montreal. You called my wife?"

"Ah, yes. That was the first thing."

They got him to a chair. A nurse came in, smiling, and spoke to the doctor in low tones. He said, "Can you come with me?" to Henri and Gus, and they all left the room. When the door opened again, Spence knew there was something. He turned to get a look. And it was Betty. Same blue eyes, the almost lean face, different dress in reality.

"Spence."

She came to him and looked and kissed him and held his head against her.

"Oh, Spence."

All he could say was "Betty." And they cried together, and laughed.

"It was just awful," she said. "The searching. And the more it went . . . Not knowing if you were alive."

"I know. I was too far north. Dumb. Nancy? and Tom?"

"They're fine. They know. I called them at work. They're coming up with Martin as soon as he can leave the hospital. I got a flight right after Henri called, I just left, like this, I couldn't wait." She passed a hand over her hair. "Tom said he always knew you'd make it."

"I figured he'd say that."

She brought over a white stool and sat on it facing him and took his hands.

"You're so skinny. And you . . . need a bath."

"I need four or five of them, and a barber."

"You have no socks."

"No." And he laughed. The man with the burning socks—that's probably what that kid said. "I burned them."

When Betty looked puzzled he added, "Probably to keep the bugs away, or maybe even to signal, I don't remember. I was pretty blank these last few days."

Silence. And then he said: "It's a good thing they came."

"You can tell me about it later. You have to take it easy."

"Yeah. Oh, yeah." But it wasn't the events he was thinking of. "You were very much there. You know, there. I was talking to you."

"That's what I was doing. Oh, Spence." And she was crying again.

"There were moments of . . . I can't quite say it yet. I'm still out there."

"It'll take time."

"Yes. Time. I've . . . come to know . . . things. I'll tell you about it when I'm ready. If I ever can."

"What sort of things?" She sounded worried for him.

"Not now. Things. It's all right. You're here, that's what matters."

"You mean *you're* here."

"It's the same thing."

She looked at him, knowing a depth, and didn't ask for a meaning. He leaned back heavily in the chair. Reentry was beginning.

246

"Martin said he wants to give you a thorough physical."

"I'm going to need it. Do you want to call that doctor back in?"

She was up immediately, saying, "What's the matter?"

"I think I'm going to pass out."

It was almost a pleasure. He was home.